EVERGREEN GIRL

by

ANNE TEDLOCK BROOKS

Author of "ISLAND NEIGHBOR,"
"THE PEACOCK FEATHER," *etc.*

Heather Nichols had been brought up in the midst of a warm and happy family in Nichols' Ferry in the Pacific Northwest. Her grandfather, Big Bill Nichols, was known and respected throughout the area and gave Heather prestige in the community; her mother gave her love and affection; her younger brother and sisters alternately worshipped and bedeviled her, and she appreciated both equally.

And yet Heather was faced with two problems: how to help keep the Nichols lumber business intact in spite of rising costs and dwindling business; and how to reconcile her liking for her neighbor, Seth Barclay, with the fact that his family was largely responsible for the Nichols family's business troubles.

A modern Romeo and Juliet seek a solution to their romance among the evergreens.

EVERGREEN GIRL

Evergreen Girl

by

ANNE TEDLOCK BROOKS

By

Sharon Publications Inc.
Cresskill, N.J.

CHAPTER 1

Big Bill Nichols was in an affable mood. A hearty dinner in the large pleasant dining room instead of out on the new flagstone terrace had contributed to his feeling of well-being.

Looking tolerantly down the table at his grandchildren and their mother, Amy, he knew that this was a rare moment. For usually the large rambling place was cluttered with droves of young people the same ages as those handsome ones at whom he now gazed so fondly.

"Gramps, you just swallowed a canary?" No one had to bother with whole quotations. Actually, they could read one another's thoughts at times. Marc, oldest of the lot, thrust up a quizzical brow at his grandfather.

"Well, I do feel a bit smug." Bill Nichols

touched the end of his grey mustache meticulously before laying down the white linen napkin monogrammed with the familiar N. Almost everyone who'd ever lived in the Bay area knew what that big, florid Victorian N stood for. "Yes, I do feel a little like the proverbial cat."

"The suspense is killing me," drawled Sam.

"Keep your pants on, young man. I've sat through the recital of enough of your activities. Anyhow, I shan't let it delay my story."

Beverly and Janet sat up a little straighter. Heather, who had been already listening attentively to her grandfather, leaned forward a bit, and a tiny crease etched itself between her straight black brows. Since her return from school she had heard a rumor or two that worried her. She knew that her mother was disturbed and that her grandfather had seemed unusually tense the past few days.

"Since this is a family affair, and since even the youngest are now old enough to understand and also to refrain from discussing it, I'm going to tell you a little of what's been going on for the past two months or so."

"Gee, Gramps!" Sam began excitedly. "I heard a huge new mill in this area was being considered."

"It's more than a rumor. But you know how we Nichols are. We wait for facts before we get excited."

Abashed, Sam subsided. At sixteen, he had a lot of other things to think about, such as his heap down the road a mile with a blow-out. And his allowance was spent and he had no money to buy a new tire.

Janet and Beverly had started to add a contribution about all the stories floating around Bayport. There was to be a ten million dollar paper mill, their cousins had told them yesterday. A planing mill, a new pulp mill, a plywood mill. Actually, their heads had reeled just thinking of all the big things about to happen. They had tried to tell their mother last evening, but she had still been busy with her church group who had spent the afternoon there.

Forthright and to the point, Bill Nichols, president of the Nichols Timber Corporation, told them quietly of the facts now known to him. "I've not bothered with fiddle-faddle. You know that in the past ten years there's been a lot of talk, but not much action, about bringing industry into the region. It takes power and raw materials and shipping facilities to take care of a really big concern.

Of course there's been groundwork going on for several years. Now we have the power. Certainly no one can deny that the forests are here, and the harbor is bound to interest Eastern money. It's happened. I learned last week that one of the largest Eastern timber operators has had an agency quietly buying up many of the small mills in the Northwest, especially in this area."

"Guess it wasn't too quietly, Grandfather," said Marc. "That was the first thing I heard when I walked down Front Street, the day I got home." Marc folded his napkin and laid it beside his dessert plate. "Paul told me the day he took me out for a ride in his new boat. Said Uncle Jonathan was doing a lot of thinking."

A steely look came into Bill Nichols' eyes. "Guess too much thinking's dangerous. Well, I've been approached to sell the Nichols' holdings. Thought I'd tell you and see how you feel about it. I'm getting well past retirement age."

"Rather!" exclaimed Sam.

"You young whippersnapper, I do as much work at seventy-five as most men do at sixty."

"You can say that again!" cried Janet loyally.

Amy Nichols reached over and patted her father-in-law's hand. "You shouldn't, you know."

Might as well tell the gulls to stop following the fishing fleet out of the harbor each morning, or tell them to stop gathering at their return to the docks when many a fish was lost in the unloading.

"I'm in semi-retirement, you know."

"Yes, we know," said Heather with amusement. "Now you work ten hours a day instead of twelve or fourteen, seven days a week. Of course, if you'd let the Jim Nichols family support itself, Gramps, instead of handing it out to us on a silver platter all these years—" she said softly.

"Your father's share provides you with a good living." The old man's voice was soft. He had never gotten over the sudden death of his older son, Jim. He didn't know how he had managed to survive the loss of both his wife and Jim within a few weeks. He had come to live at Nichols' Ferry with Amy and the children after a long siege of pneumonia had almost taken him, too. It was easier to stay with them, in spite of all the confusion, than to live on alone in the neat small house in town. Without Elizabeth, who had been married to him for forty years, he had faced life with reluctance until he came out to the country place to convalesce.

"Grandpa, you're not really thinking of selling

out?" Marc asked in a low voice. "We'd respect your judgment, but, sir, I've looked forward to coming back here and going into this business with everything I've got. And as I told you the other evening, I'm 'loaded for bear.' "

Nichols nodded agreeably. "And I'm keeping your plans uppermost in my mind, Marc. I'm not going off half-cocked and sell the means of a very fine livelihood. Oh, I know business dropped off a lot during the depression. But since the war, we've had more orders than we can fill. Ships from every port that we used to sell to, and other places as well, have been increasing their orders. The only thing is, if our supply is cut off, we may have to spend more money getting out production, and we're going to have to get on the ball."

"Shall we have a meeting right away?" asked Marc.

"Yes. I've called one for tomorrow at three. Jon and Paul can be there. I want Heather and Amy and you to be at my office at two-thirty. I'm not going to rush you, of course, but I do want you to think about it. Jan and Beverly and Sam are under age, but I want their opinions, too."

"Gosh, Granddad, all I've ever known is the Timber Corporation." Sam's voice faltered a little.

"I can tell you right now that if it was mine, I'd never sell it."

"Count me in on that, too," cried Beverly. "You, too, Jan?"

Janet nodded gravely, her short curly hair making a pale halo around her oval face. She leaned over and put her hand on top of her twin's. They were so much alike you had to hunt for the chicken pox scar above Jan's left eyebrow to be sure of their identification. "I don't want ever to know any other kind of life."

"This is plenty good enough for me," agreed Sam.

Amy Nichols laughed, and her soft voice silenced the others. "It's been an ultra special kind of life, Ducklings. You've never really wanted much in the way of material things that you didn't get. Actually, if Gramps hadn't helped me keep you straightened out, you'd all be spoiled rotten, and you know it."

"Like Paul and Babs," sniffed Beverly.

"Nothing wrong with Babs that a good hard spanking wouldn't have taken care of while she was still young enough," said Marc. "As for Paul, he's okay, and don't get any other ideas."

Heather looked at him. Their blue eyes met, and

Marc grinned. You couldn't fool Heather. She was the one whose name should be in gold on a *Vice-President, Private* sign on the office door. Just because she was a girl was no sign that she'd no head for business. Gramps knew it, too.

"There are many things to consider," Heather said. "Not only might we have to increase our payroll, buy up more timberlands, hang on with dog-like tenacity, but we also have to consider if it would be better financially to sell. Too, we have to reflect that Marc's just out of school, Sam's a long way from commencement, and I'm not much good in an office. You're the one with the know-how, Gramps, and I think it's time you were considering letting someone else take over your hard work."

"I'm planning on Marc's filling my place. In fact, he's taking over a desk tomorrow morning in the office next to Jon's." He turned to his oldest grandson. "Paul had it all fixed up today. The painters got through yesterday, and he had that new desk and the chairs and a few other things moved in. I was going to tell you about it earlier."

"Just got in from Siletz after six, Gramps." Marc's voice was warm with eagerness. "Gee! I appreciate all the new fixings."

His grandfather brushed this aside. "How was

everything at Camp Forty? Did you see the fore-
man?" He rose, and the others knew that the family
parley was over. He and Marc moved toward the
study, and the remaining members began to scatter.

The twins went to the game room to pick up
their tennis racquets, and Sam slammed a side door
as he went out to the garage. His big dog, Queenie,
a handsome collie who could have doubled for
Lassie, bounded at his heels with little playful yelps.

Situated about six miles out of the town of Bayport, on the Yaquina River, the place known to all
the area as Nichols' Ferry basked in the quiet of a
beautiful sunset. In the bend of the river, its two
hundred acres, part of which had been "patented"
during the term of President Arthur, were hand-
somely cared for.

On the rolling foothills of the Coast Range the
big herd of Guernseys fed. The Nichols employed
a man and his wife full-time for gardening and
housework, and a part-time maid came in twice a
week for general cleaning.

The house was huge and rambling, with added
wings and ells and porches and patios; all in good
taste and having the appearance of a deep South
mansion with growing pains. Well-protected from
the Pacific, which was but a scant five miles away

by boat through the channel, the grounds were beautifully landscaped.

Rhododendrons, mock orange, native huckleberry, salal, kinnekinick, spruce, firs and juniper provided constant greenery which was the envy of all guests.

Gramps' father, Elias Nichols, had come from England in the eighties, bringing a small fortune to invest in a railroad which had prospered for a time on the Coast. He had been canny enough to buy timberlands and to set up one of the first sawmills on Sally's Slough. His first cottage had stood where the big stables now stood, back in a small cove about a quarter of a mile from the main house. He had bought the ferryboat, the *Oneatta*, from one of the older citizens and for a time had run it himself. Old Cap'n Nichols had had a good business head. Respected and admired for his achievements, he added to his small fortune and, at the time of his death, left a goodly inheritance to his sons, Jonathon and William. They sold all their father's holdings except the timber and his sawmills, built a larger mill about eight miles upriver and became partners in it.

During World War I, the Government bought vast quantities of spruce and fir from them. Their company became known as one of the largest spruce mills in the world. They furnished lumber for planes and ships, army barracks and general construction.

During this time, they added huge tracts of forest land to their holdings, and built a small railway into the wilderness to haul out giant logs. When the war ended, however, building dropped to a minimum and the Nichols Corporation began to retrench. They sold many of their smaller sawmills on isolated creeks and closed up logging camps in the Siletz area, for their ponds were filled with water-soaked logs and the saw logs were stacked up to fabulous heights awaiting the blades of giant knives.

Big Bill Nichols used frequently to awaken from a nightmare, drenched with perspiration, after dreaming of losing everything. The following morning, he'd tell his sons that he was thankful they'd not bought the freighters which had been offered them just before the close of the war.

"If there has been any one factor which has contributed to our success in the lumber business," he would say, "it was careful planning in running our operation, and never going into debt to such an extent that we could lose the business. We had no need for those freighters as long as the buyers were paying their bills and were glad to get the lumber."

Jonathon was impatient with his father at times. He was not like Jim, who had plodded along and died of a cerebral hemorrhage at fifty-six. Jim had sat up late at night poring over books and worrying about production and the lack of sales. The thirties had been a time of agonizing idleness. It seemed as though they just waited for bankruptcy to strike.

"No, we're holding our own," Jim would say.

"The heck with it! I'm going to take my kids on a decent vacation. I'm going to send Sue to Europe with her friends. What do I care how little or how much we make this year? Dad always comes through if we need money."

"I don't think I'd let Sue go to Europe, Jon," Jim had said one day after an outburst in the early spring of 1938. "There's a lot of unrest. Europe's a hot spot, ready to bust out at any time."

"Why kid ourselves? She's waited long enough."

"Why don't you go with her, then? If you don't have the money, I'll lend it to you, and we'll keep Babs and Paul while you're gone. The kids would have a wonderful time."

"You're a nice guy, Jim. I may do that," Jon had answered.

CHAPTER 2

Heather was lost in thought as she went upstairs to her room. She sat down on the chaise near the open windows and looked out upon the quiet green lawn below. If her grandfather really needed to get away from the lumber business, would Marc be able to handle it, with Paul's help? Paul, though older and more experienced, since he'd been in a supervisor's office for three years, was not as level-headed as her brother. Paul was apt to be carried away by impulse and to act without consulting his grandfather.

Heather, looking back on their childhood, realized that Paul had usually been the one who had led them into scrapes, and that Marc was the one who had gotten them out. Like a vivid pattern of a vast mosaic, the years at Nichols' Ferry spread themselves across her memory.

It had all begun when Jonathon's children came to stay with Jim's family, here in the country.

That was one of the happier times in the two brothers' relationship. Sue and Jonathon had gone to Europe and left their two children at the James Nicholses' home at the Ferry Landing. Paul was five and Barbara seven. Heather and Marc were four and six. The four children had had a picnic. The twins and Sam hadn't yet arrived to bless the Jim Nichols home.

Time dragged on, and Sue and Jonathon stayed on in Paris and then in Italy, where it was warm during the winter months. They were actually gone a year, lacking six weeks. Forced to come home because of the approach of World War II, Sue told Amy she was anxious to see her children. "But it's such a pokey life compared to life abroad," she confided. "Really, Amy, I don't see how you stand such a humdrum existence."

"Nothing humdrum about life at the Ferry," Amy had replied with a smile. "Oh, I get tired, and I get disgusted now and then because the power fails and we have to light lamps all over the place and cook on oil stoves, but I do enjoy my family."

Even then, she knew she'd said the wrong thing. A year later, in spite of the war and the unrest, Sue

had gone East for a visit with a friend, and she had
never returned to Bayport.

"Confidentially, Amy, I think it contributed to
Elizabeth's death. It hurt her so to see Paul and Babs
deserted by their mother without a regret. I had no
idea things had gone that far. Oh, I knew that Jon
and Sue were not getting along, but I'd hoped
that their trip would cure that," Big Bill had said.

Secretly, Amy thought the trip had just added
to Sue's restlessness.

Talking to his son Jim, Bill Nichols had said,
"Sue's never been the girl that your Amy is. Coming from a little town, she does give herself airs.
Now your wife's always been steady and dependable and made a good home for the children and
you. Sue's been on the rampage ever since I gave
her her first car. I should never have done it. Used
to complain that she couldn't go anywhere because
of lack of transportation, and Dad blame it! I could
never find her home after she got a car. Jon's
sending her alimony and she's spending it faster
than he can make it. He's a fool."

Amy had been inclined to agree with her father-
in-law. They heard from Sue spasmodically, and
one winter, Barbara went East to be with her
mother. Jon found out that Sue had put her in a

private school when Babs wrote about how homesick she was, a little girl of nine.

Barbara wrote begging her father to come and get her, or to send her money so that she could come home. Paul was the one who sent it.

His scrawling writing said, "*Dear Babs, Here's enough money to catch the train. You don't haf to stay at that crummy place. I've been saving my lowance since I read your letter last month. Marc and Heather gave me some of there's two. Come on home. The water's swell, and the boat's ready to launch. We named her the Sea Spright. Your pony's going to have a colt. Gramps is real mad at Mommie. And I am two.*"

All the Nichols children remembered, with varying degrees of emotion, the time that Babs had run away from school.

It had caused quite a commotion.

The only ones who knew that she was coming home to Bayport were Paul, Heather and Marc. They hitched up their ponies and took the cart into town to meet the train. Paul was staying with them while their father was out of town on business; he was due home the same day as Babs. It was a warm December seventh. The Christmas decorations had been hung crisscross above the streets and the lights turned on early, for there was fog.

The train pulled in and Barbara Nichols, an eager little figure, was the first one off the steps. She and Heather hurled themselves into each other's arms and kissed and cried. Paul said, "For Pete's sake, do you have to make so much over nothing?"

Marc, embarrassed, said, "You better hurry now, 'cause it's gettin' dark. Where's your baggage and stuff?"

"I didn't bring anything but just myself and this little case. They can send the rest to me."

"Weren't you scared coming all alone?"

"Of course not! You forget I traveled East by myself last fall."

"I'm surprised that Mom let you come."

"She didn't. I just ran away."

The other three children stared in amazement. Barbara had managed everything so adroitly that they couldn't believe she had actually run away, although they had most certainly provided her with transportation money. She had written them not to tell her father or any of the other grown-ups so it could be a surprise. Since Nichols' Ferry was a constant treasury of surprises, they had followed her suggestion.

They were silent as they walked to the cart. Just before they reached the tethered ponies, they saw a cluster of older boys coming out of a pool room.

"I'm signing up tomorrow. The yellow-bellied sneaks!" said one of the boys in a loud voice. "We'll be in the war tomorrow."

"What'll your Dad say?"

"Not much. I flunked out this last year anyway. How about you, Mike? Coming with me? I'm going to try to get into the Air Force."

"You think we're going to have a war?" Heather asked Paul.

"Of course," he said nonchalantly.

"Yes, we are," said Barbara. "A man got on at the last station. He talked real loud and said we'd been bombed at Pearl Harbor." Her voice was a little shaky. "Do you think Daddy will have to go?"

Paul said gravely, "He might. But maybe he's too old."

Jonathon arrived home from Portland almost frantic. He had received a wire that Barbara had disappeared from school. He had talked with his former wife, and Sue had cried over the telephone. It had shaken him a great deal, though it didn't make sense that Sue should be really concerned about Barbara.

He begged Sue to return to Bayport. She said that she might, and pleaded with him to come East and help find his daughter.

He called his brother's house to tell Jim that he was leaving immediately for the East and learned that Babs and the rest of them were just sitting down to dinner. Thirteen minutes later Jonathon stood, shaken and pale, in the dining room door.

"Why didn't someone bother to let me know?" he asked furiously.

"But, Jon," Amy protested, "you were in Portland. We didn't know that you were back."

"Barbara, you ran away! I'm going to whip you within an inch of your life!"

Amy rose swiftly, went over to him and said, "Wait, Jon. She's just been here a few minutes. Poor little girl. Let me talk to you, Jonny!"

"Scaring us to death! Your poor mother!" Jon shouted at Barbara.

"Sue?" There was so much scorn in Amy's quiet tone that Jon's head shot back in amazement. Gentle Amy, who had never offered one word of condemnation against Sue!

"She cried over the phone."

Amy, white with anger, laid her hand on his sleeve. "Maybe she *was* frightened, Jon." Barbara was crying silently. Jim rose and came over to them.

"Why don't you let Amy handle this, Jon?" he

said. "You're much too upset right now. Why don't you sit down and have supper with us?"

"Don't interfere with me and my daughter," Jon said indignantly.

"You're overacting the scene, Jon," said Amy. "Don't overplay the part; for really, neither you nor Sue have acted like parents in the past three years. Now if you think I'm going to stand by and see Barbara paddled for something you and Sue should be spanked for, you're mistaken. The only crying Sue's done for three or four years has been for more money to spend, and you know it."

"You're criticizing my wife," Jon shouted.

"Your former wife," she corrected him. "Do be sensible, and come into the study and let me tell you what happened."

"You didn't care that half the police in New York City are out looking for you," Jon said to Barbara, ignoring Amy.

"Oh, come now; Babs left a note in her room. Sue just played it up. I don't want to upset the children; come along and let's talk this out. Better yet, let me set you a place. Maybe you'd better wire Sue, if you think she's really worried about Babs."

"Well," Jon said, "I did have enough sense to call in a wire that Babs had come home." Jon looked over at Barbara and his face softened a little.

Amy stepped back to the table and rang a little silvery bell. "Bring in a plate for Mr. Jonathon," she said to the cook. "Do sit down, Jon, right beside me."

"I'll just have some coffee, if you don't mind."

She poured it for him. Barbara and Paul went back home with their father a half-hour later.

Heather remembered her father's quiet words to her mother: "Don't worry about it, dear. After all, Jon knows that you were telling the truth, and in case you think you were out of line, let me tell you that Dad's been giving Jon the devil. Sue didn't really care about Barbara leaving. She'll try to get her back, but only because of the income which goes with her."

"How can anyone be so cruel?" Amy asked tearfully. "Jim, if he punishes Babs tonight, he'll never be welcome in our house again."

"Oh, now, Amy, you mustn't say things like that."

With a spirit that a casual observer would never have suspected existed within her, Amy Nichols said, "I do mean it. I've never been more serious. Paul's and Barbara's welfare means as much to me as do my own children's. Poor little kids, they have had no real home for a long time."

Heather, overhearing all this, had cried bitterly for Barbara. If her Uncle Jon punished her cousin, she told herself, she would never forgive him. He did not punish her, but he did make her go back to school in the East.

And that was so much worse than a spanking that Heather could never bring herself really to love him again. Barbara, a sad little girl, came home for good at Christmas a year later, and no one could ever get her to leave for an Eastern school again, though Heather went to Bryn Mawr; and the boys, Paul and Marc, attended Harvard.

Jonathon went East three times, hoping for a reconciliation with Sue, but one never came off, and she remarried six years later. This time her husband was a surgeon in Philadelphia; a successful man who was respected for his work and had an excellent practice among the socially elite. Heather, when she visited her aunt in the East, found her a changed woman. Sue was quietly engrossed in philanthropic works which kept her busy spending with a free hand the lavish contributions made by her associates. Her husband was the head of his household, and Sue respected his authority and bowed to it.

CHAPTER 3

Presently Heather went downstairs to join her mother. Mrs. Nichols had been discussing the canning of fifty pounds of tuna brought in unexpectedly by the skipper of a large lumber barge which carried cargoes of finished lumber to the docks across the Bay. When not piloting the barge, old Captain Sneed operated a commercial fishing boat, the *Skalliwag*, and provided fellow employees and his superiors with plenty of tuna for their lockers and their shelves of canned goods.

Coming into the living room, Amy Nichols sank down gratefully on the green sofa. "All that tuna would come in just as we're needed downtown tomorrow afternoon. I have a luncheon at one o'clock, too."

"Don't worry about the fish, Mother. After all

these years, Sarah should be capable of handling it."

"She is. Sarah comes through in every emergency. It's rough on her. I think I'll give her a month off this year to go visit her daughter in Yoncalla."

"Why not? But do pick a time when she's not up to her neck freezing fruit, canning berries or making jelly, or we'll be buried in the kitchen," suggested Heather. "Remember that time two years ago when she had to go help Rachel have her baby?"

"One experience is enough! Of all the times—right in the busiest period of the year. Poor Sarah! I don't see how she's stood all of us Nicholses through the years."

Heather smiled. Sarah was a bulwark against storm and strife.

"Why don't we go and join Marc and Grandpa?" she suggested. "Otherwise they'll talk business most of the night."

"Really, they've not had much chance to discuss any problems, other than those of immediate concern. Heather, I'm really worried about this other big mill coming into the area. My bridge club was talking about it last week. Actually, I've known that the smog around this place has been getting worse as production has increased since the war, but we have managed to keep it within bounds. Have you ever thought what would happen if a huge plant is operated in this area?"

"Yes. I've been to Pittsburgh and Wheeling and have seen some of the smoke-blackened buildings. Of course there are a number of ways to take care of smoke today, Mother. Doubtless the new plant will be able to keep it down."

"We've all been a little lethargic around here. The depression cut down industry, but almost everyone went his placid way, barely making a living, but enjoying the peace and quiet of the Coast."

"Gone Hunting," quoted Heather, remembering the signs to be found on shop windows during deer season. "Be back after Thanksgiving!"

They laughed, and her mother said, "It is a sort of comical existence, come to think of it, but healthful. Where else does one live to be ninety-four?" She referred to an elderly friend of her grandfather's, one of the men who had come from England with his own father in the eighties.

"Shall I make some lemonade?" asked Heather. "It's a bit warm tonight, and you know how Grandfather is."

"Yes, do. And call Janet and Beverly in when you're through. They must get to bed at a decent hour, and I know they'll want to bathe and probably to shampoo their hair tonight. They're off early tomorrow on a trip with the Hamiltons."

"Where to this time?"

"To Portland to see the Rose Parade. Big day ahead of them. They're leaving at five. Can you imagine getting them up? But they'll set the alarm for four-thirty and be out at the highway in time."

"I remember when I was seventeen," Heather said wistfully. "Everything was so important. Everything was beautiful or tragic or sordid or heavenly. Nothing was halfway. The ultimate in everything." She struck up a pose in the doorway, her slender body slightly bent to one side, her eyes closed as if in ecstasy.

"Don't remind me. Two at a time are enough!" said Amy. "And don't forget Sam!" she called after her daughter.

"Who ever could?" Heather's voice wafted back laughingly.

She could hear his off-note whistle as he came across the side lawn, calling to the twins, now sitting on a stone bench wistfully gazing out at the Pacific, where they could see the white of the breakers across the bar.

It's good to be back home, she thought, touching the shining maple paneling in the wide hall, rubbing her fingers over the smooth wood caressingly. Oh, I know you're not elegant, you old house, but I love you. I love every crack in the plaster and every brick in your chimneys, and every worn threshold in the place. Every time one of the family got the notion to sell the place or to tear it down and build a new one, there were shrieks of outraged indignation. Usually something new would be added, or some part of the house would be redecorated to placate the whim of the one who had suggested the change. Usually, too, the whim would long since have been forgotten by the time the new work was completed.

"Nope, you never gain but what you lose something, I always say," old Captain Sneed would tell them. "Now look what you've gone and done—spoiled that purty rose bed of your grandma's. I've seen her many a time, with her white gloves on, going to a party, reach down and pull out a plagued weed. No, sir, you'll not get roses like them again soon! And serve you right, too!"

The ramblers over the stable entrance and the purple and white clematis over the old kitchen porch were in full bloom. They had been Grandma's, too, and Bill Nichols tended to cutting them back every year. No one else dared touch them.

Heather paused in the doorway of the vast kitchen. It was little like the original, except that they had left a huge fireplace in the middle of the room. Now beautiful steel built-in cabinets, ranges and refrigerators graced the walls, and the big new dishwasher was quietly taking care of the china and glassware from the dinner table.

A small, plump, grey-haired woman sat in a rocking chair hulling peas for the locker. She looked up and smiled at her favorite.

"I'm going to make some lemonade, Sarah. Would you and Nels like some, too?" Heather asked.

"I'm sure Nels would, for he's out working in the strawberries, but none for me, please. I'm thinking of that new dress your mother's making me. I want to wear it to church next Sunday, and it's a mite close-fitting."

"Don't you get the dieting bug, Sarah!" Heather stood by her chair a moment and patted one soft shoulder. "You're just right, and besides, where'd you get the energy to cope with all of us if you didn't eat properly?"

"Don't worry, honey. I'll cope all right. I've got

a new scheme cooked up, as Sam would say. Everyone takes care of his own linens this summer. Once a week they bring down their sheets and towels ready for washing and they put them in. Too many beds in this household for me to look after in the summertime."

"I'll remember. What is my day for laundry?"

"Better make it Friday morning. You put 'em in, and I'll take them out when they're dry and fold them. They don't get ironed unless the person who uses them runs them through the ironer. I noticed the twins have slacked off. The first week they were neat as pins. But now I have to remind them to take the linen back to the linen closet in their bathroom."

"I know. We're an ungrateful lot, Sarah. But don't ever leave us."

"Don't worry, Heather. Like Captain Sneed reminds me, I've got it good. Nels and I both know that. We've never wanted for anything since coming to work for your pa and ma, and we've a tidy bank account and plenty of spare time during slack seasons."

Heather, running lemons through the squeezer, smiled. "What season is slack around Nichols' Ferry?"

"Oh, when the younguns are all at school, and

it's raining and no work can be done outside, Nels and I sit here snug as bugs, drinking coffee and playing gin rummy. Your grandpa taught us that the winter he came to live here."

"He's a character, a lovely dear character!"

"Yes, he is, and one of the finest men that ever lived."

" 'We belong to a Mutual Admiration Society,' " sang Heather to herself as she added water and sugar to the juice.

Getting out the ice and filling the glasses, Heather finished with a flourish and then cleaned up the counter with a sponge. Sarah had long since taught the Nichols children that if they used her kitchen for snack making they had to clean up their messes. As a last touch, Heather broke off some sprigs of mint and added them to the glasses. She paused at the side door, going down the hall with the tray in her hand, and called to the girls:

"Lemonade! Come and get it!"

Like leaping gazelles, they loped across the lawn, long tanned legs flashing under their tennis shorts, fair hair shining in the last rays of the sun.

"You're a livin' doll!" shouted Sam, sprinting from the garage, a streak of black across his forehead, his fingers smudging the sides of the glass. "Don't tell me; I know this one's for me." He hesitated. "I s'pose this one's for Nels? I'll take it to him."

"Right. Well, I'll see you later. Girls, Mother said it's almost time for you to do your nightly chores, if you're getting up early. What stamina! I remember the last Rose Parade I saw. I couldn't walk for two days, I was so exhausted."

"But we got friends this year. Stephanie is one of the Princesses. We get a special seat." Janet smiled smugly.

Stephanie Moore had originally lived at Bayport, but had moved to Portland and attended one of the large high schools. Secretly the twins envied her the city life she enjoyed, but she always seemed happy to visit them at Nichols' Ferry.

"She's coming home with us if we stay over. We still have to persuade Mother. Help us, won't you, Heather? There's a real dreamy dance tomorrow night at the Country Club, and we'd like to stay all night."

Heather winked at them. "I'll see what I can do for you, if you'll come on in in a few minutes without being called. Mother's pretty upset about the mill, you know."

"I should say she is! A lot more than you think!" said Sam.

"What do you know about it, Kids? After all,

I've been gone ten months."

"Well, it's going to be pretty bad if that big new timber company does all the things we heard they plan on doing. And it looks to me like they're big enough to swallow up all the little gyppo mills around the country. Most of them have closed down. Some of them didn't even open up after the fire season last fall. And don't let Grandpa fool you. He's known what's going on all the time. He just hates to admit it." Sam twisted his tennis shoe around in the grass. "How do you feel about selling out, Sis?"

"I've got to know more about it. My first reaction was never to sell. But we've got to think clearly and not be sentimental. After all, we'd probably make quite a lot on the transaction."

"But it would be so final. And there are a lot more people involved now than forty years ago when Grandpa and Great-Uncle Jon took over."

"A lot more complications, too, Sam."

"Yes, but it's a going concern, and it's going great, if you ask me. Get Marc to show you some of the annual reports, Heather. They'll show you what I mean."

"Looks to me that you've a pretty good idea yourself. How come you know so much about the business?"

"Grandpa'd talk to me evenings this winter after I got through with my homework. He's really something, Sis."

"Yes, I know."

"Don't ever underestimate Grandpa's ability," said Sam seriously. "Personally, I'd like to go into the business myself. Paul doesn't care much for it, but Marc and I can make a go of it. That is, if we don't let it go to pot now that we have competitors in the field."

"Don't be silly, Sam. Nobody's going to let the Nichols Timber Corporation go to pot!" Marc's deep voice boomed out.

"Well, of course not, Marc!" Heather's voice placated him.

"Private conclave, or can anybody get into this?" their older brother asked.

"I would like to have a talk with you alone after Mom's in bed, Marc. And without Grandpa around, too. We've got to discuss this before tomorrow."

"Right. I'd planned on getting you to go out to try the new station wagon after we have the lemonade." Marc helped himself to a glass. "Grandpa's waiting for his, impatiently."

She nodded. "I'll serve them, and then join you in the drive."

In the living room, her grandfather took his glass from the proffered tray. "Marc said he's taking you for a ride. Tell him to take it easy on those new curves, the ones up over Otter Crest."

"Okay, Grandpa, we'll be careful."

"By the way, I'm having new tires put on your little car this week."

"I'll try to earn them, Gramps. When are you going to let me go to work for you? I can take dictation, you know, and type a pretty good letter."

"We'll see. First of all, I want you to have a vacation. Plenty of time later to go to work. Isn't there a young man in the offing? What happened to that roommate of your brother's?" Grandfather sipped his lemonade. "Mercer?"

"Hal?" Heather's voice seemed casual. "Oh, he had other interests. There was a girl in New York. You remember, don't you, Mother?"

Her mother could always be counted on. "Yes, I do believe Hal mentioned her when he was here last summer with Marc."

"I was hoping you'd hit it off, Heather. I liked him," Grandpa said. "Had a good head on him, just like your brother. Smart fellow, and bound to go places."

"Yes, I know." But he'd already chosen the girl to go with him, and she didn't happen to be Heather. "And now, Cupid," she smiled at her grandfather; "I'll run along. We may stop at the Hi-Tide on our way back."

CHAPTER 4

Marc, seated in the big new station wagon, was waiting for Heather in the drive at the side of the house. The engine was purring softly and the door was open. She stepped in and they rolled down the incline. The twins waved, and Sam hurled insults playfully.

"No place like Nichols' Ferry," murmured Heather.

"You can say that again!"

"I often do." Heather rolled down the window and drank thirstily of the salt air. "Gee! It's wonderful to be home."

Her brother nodded. "I was anxious to get back; Sam wrote me about the mill. He's pretty upset about it, too. You know, he doesn't think much of Paul's ability."

"How do you feel?"

"I think he's flubbed a few times, but then his heart's not really in it. Uncle Jon wouldn't let him study medicine, and you know he wanted to."

"He should have done it anyway. These days you don't obey your parents to the letter if it interferes with your future."

"But you know Uncle Jon; he wouldn't have given him a dollar for school. Paul had to have the money. He's making the best of things."

"Seriously, how are things at the mills?"

Marc lit a cigarette. "I'm not absolutely certain, but I think something's being held back. I don't think even Grandpa knows that the company still owes the Government for the last Liberty ship we bought. Uncle Jonathon evidently let him think it was given to us just to get rid of it, but there's more to it than that. I ran across a statement, but Grandpa's never mentioned the note. There are other things too, that need to be gone through with a fine-toothed comb. Prosperity that is false isn't real prosperity."

"What do you mean?"

"That's not all profit that we're getting from those huge shipments of lumber which leave port three times a week. There's a big payroll; damage and repairs and other overhead seem to be taking their toll."

"But Sam says it looks wonderful."

"Sam's a kid."

"He seems to have studied the annual reports, which I've not seen."

"I'll level with you, Sis. Grandpa's worried about the new mills. He thinks they're going to run all of the small concerns out of business and get a monopoly if we're not careful. It's up to us, if we don't sell to Pacific Timber, to hold on like bulldogs. But we have to do a lot of considering and a lot of figuring."

Marc pulled up at Lookout Point. "Thought I'd like to go into it a bit more, and then we'll pick up Paul and let you judge for yourself on the basis of what he says. There were definite undertones when we had our first talk."

"How do you think he feels about selling?"

"He wants to sell."

"Just like that?"

"Oh, there's a lot more to it. He's worked for three years next to Uncle Jon and Grandpa. He's third in rank, you know. He says we'd be smart to ask our price and get out from under."

"Under what?"

"He doesn't really say."

"Marc, do you think there's been anything underhanded about this whole affair?"

Her brother didn't answer for a long moment. "Paul's always been square in little things with us, Heather. You know that. If things have happened, I'll wager that Uncle Jon's responsible for them, and that he went over Paul's head. He isn't really a very good businessman."

"He's pretty stupid to stay in an office when he hates it."

"Oh, I can't say he hates it. But he just isn't inspired."

"And you? Does the prospect of perhaps running Nichols Timber by yourself some day inspire you, Marc? Of course Sam will be old enough to help in a few years."

"Six, at least. That's a long time. But I'd rather be in timber than anything else. You forget that I grew up in the woods, spent weeks at a time in the forests at the camps near Siletz. Lord! I wouldn't even mind being a logger."

"I guess you wouldn't!" Heather patted his brown hand. She looked at him fondly. Dark brown hair, deep blue eyes and a well built body. He was a real Nichols; he resembled the pictures of the family, some on walls in gold frames, and some in big family albums in chests in the attic. She couldn't imagine their family being in any kind of business other than timber. With three younger children yet to be educated, and about twelve people involved, they simply couldn't afford to give up the business at this point.

"You'd like to keep the business, wouldn't you, Marc?"

He nodded.

"So would I, unless there's danger of going broke."

"Oh, it's not nearly that bad, Heather. I think there are some payments due right away, and I know there's money to cover them. I'm going to bring them up at the directors' meeting tomorrow and get out from under on them." Marc started the engine. The waters of the Pacific had now purpled into darkness, and they could see the channel lights flashing in the harbor.

"Why don't we have it out with Paul tonight?"

"I don't know if it's the time or place. He could smooth things over with us, but not with Grandpa. It may be an advantage to spring it on him tomorrow when he's not expecting it. I doubt if Paul or Uncle Jon know that I'm aware of the situation."

Marc drove into the town of Bayport; crossing Front Street and following a tree-lined, curving boulevard, he drew up beside a large, impressive stone house. Two cars stood in the drive and young voices floated out of the living room.

"Looks like Babs has company. Maybe Paul, too," Heather said.

"He'd have called me. Shall I go in and get him?" Marc slipped out from the seat and crossed the terrace to the front door. He pressed the chimes and Barbara came to the door.

"Is Paul ready? He's going to help me and Heather try out the new car. Can you come along?"

"Thanks, Marc. I've a carload of company here from Corvallis. Come in?"

"No, I'll just wait here for Paul."

"I'm coming down, Marc," his cousin called from upstairs. Leaning out of the window, Paul waved a hand.

A few minutes later the station wagon rolled out of town toward the new highway over Otter Crest. Marc drove rather slowly at first, then faster as they left the suburbs. It was a cool night, and the windows were open; Heather felt the strong breeze blowing through her dark curls.

"Sure nice to have you home, Coz," Paul said earnestly. His arm around her shoulders tightened a bit. "I missed you last winter; you and Marc, too. Gosh, things get a little gruesome during the rainy season."

"It's nice to be back, Paul. I always love to get home in the summer. Just one more term."

They talked a little about school and about the things one could do in New York over the weekend.

"Makes me feel like an old man, hearing about Marc's commencement," said Paul, lighting his pipe.

"You still smoking that old smelly thing?" asked Heather.

"You're speaking of the pipe I love, I'll remind you."

Heather laughed and burrowed her head into his shoulder. How silly of them to think Paul would do anything questionable. She could never doubt his integrity. "Paul, I hate to bring up business our first visit together, but I'd sure like you to tell us what you know about the new mills."

"Well—" Paul's voice deepened. His executive voice. Heather recalled, smiling to herself, that the twins had called attention to the change that took place in his voice when he spoke on business matters, and the contrast with his ordinary speaking voice. "Well, it's like this. Pacific Timber is a huge concern. Holdings all over America, with the exception of the Northwest, until this year. They have rather quietly begun to buy up a lot of medium-sized mills, and then during the past few weeks, some very large ones up in Washington. Frankly, they're out to form a dynasty."

"But the government won't allow a monopoly."

"Right. But the next thing to a monopoly can operate long enough to throw us out of the works. Squeezing us out will be easy if we can't get labor."

"Why would we lose our labor?" she asked.

"They might offer more money," Marc suggested.

"Some of that sort of thing is managed by the unions, of course, but we can get squeezed out easily enough. It seems to me that we should seriously consider their offer."

"You mean there's been an honest bona fide offer to buy?"

"Well, of course! You didn't think all these rumors were just for fun, did you? Dad's coming in from Mexico tomorrow in time for the meeting. He'll have some important things to say, so I hope his plane's not late."

"If you know what they are, Paul, why not tell us? After all, we're family first, and business associates afterwards, I hope," Heather said. "It will help if we're able to think about them and don't have to make any decisions on the spur of the moment."

Paul smoked silently.

"Come now, Heather; no one's going to rush you into a decision," chided Marc.

Heather gave him a little pinch for stepping into the breach of silence that Paul had created. Why didn't Paul tell them everything? Why shouldn't they know? After all, they were a part of the corporation, too. There were others: The president of the bank, two of the port commissioners and three other members of the firm. The largest stockholders, of course, were the members of the Nichols family and they could cast a deciding vote.

"No use to bother your pretty little head, Heather," Paul said, patting her shoulder.

"Even Grandfather doesn't belittle my business acumen like that, Paul Nichols," she said with spirit, shrugging off his hand. "I'd like to know what it's all about. Come now, and give us your reasons for being worried."

"Did I say that I'm worried about anything?"

"Only that you think we might get squeezed out, to quote you verbatim."

"We can ask a price."

"You want to sell, don't you, Paul?" Heather asked.

"I think it would be for the best of all concerned."

"Why?"

"Many reasons, too numerous to mention, and some you wouldn't understand."

"It might interest you to know that I've taken some business administration along with my secretarial courses." Heather's voice was firm.

Marc swerved the car toward the turn-around and headed back toward Bayport. He said chidingly, "It's a heck of a pretty night. Can't you two people discuss something more interesting? I'm pretty bored."

"Oh, hush, Marc."

"If you think you're going to get any business secrets out of your cousin tonight, you're wrong, Sis. He's got personal integrity. His restraint is remarkable, and you ought to be ashamed of yourself. Let up, won't you? Paul," Marc said with laughter in his voice, "I wish you'd been with me today. I met up with those two characters we worked with one summer in the woods up by Camp 40. You remember them, Bus and Ed? Haven't changed a bit. Thought of you while I was talking with them. Remember that chaw of terbaccer Bus fixed you up with?"

Paul groaned. "Don't mention it. I get sick every time I think of it. Those were the good old days; wouldn't you like to relive them?"

Marc started to answer, but stopped. Heather knew he'd been about to refer to the complications at the mill. She said nothing. If Paul wanted to play games, she knew two who could match him point for point: Marc and herself. They'd rehearse what they'd say at the meeting tomorrow. Marc would know how to present his discovery in a way that would completely change the picture. Grandpa would be furious, of course. But then, she smiled, she had seen him furious a number of times in her life.

CHAPTER 5

They didn't stop at the Hi-Tide night club, but went directly back home after dropping their cousin. Lights were still on in the upstairs bedrooms, and their mother was still in the living room.

"I'm glad you came home early," Amy said to her oldest children. "We've not really had much chance to visit since your return. Would you like coffee?"

"Maybe a little later, Mother," said Heather. "If we do, I'll make some. We've been talking to Paul, and Marc and I think you ought to know how we feel about things, because it will help us to be a little better prepared tomorrow. Really, Marc, I think you should have told Grandpa about the note on that freighter."

"What are you talking about?" Amy asked.

"Freighter? I guess I really don't know much about what's been going on, if there's any big debt hanging over the company." She looked tired tonight, Heather suddenly noted. "It's been generally understood that we kept out of heavy indebtedness because of Grandfather's earlier experiences. He's been very conservative all these years; that's undoubtedly why we've been able to make such profits since World War II."

"Did you attend any of the directors' meetings last winter?" Marc asked.

"No, I'm afraid not. There was always something. Uncle Jon said it really wasn't necessary. Even Grandpa didn't go to them all. He had the flu in December, and was still weak in January. He went," she paused, "in March, I believe it was, and of course since then he's attended regularly. A meeting a month does slip up on one, you know. My bridge club meets on the same day, and I do get involved." Sudden guilt sounded in her voice. "But Dad Nichols always had a report of the minutes, you can be certain."

"Don't look so stricken, Mom. It may not be of any importance, but I've got a thing or two to say tomorrow if it looks as though a wrong decision will be made."

They talked a while longer and then went to the kitchen for hot cocoa instead of coffee.

Heather slept fairly well, in spite of her perturbation lest the big industry she had known all her life be sold out of the family. Determined to fight the sale if it seemed best, she needed to bolster her energy. Awaking at seven, she saw that it would be a lovely day.

She showered and put on clamdiggers and a cotton knit sweater for the morning, intending to give anyone a lift with whatever work needed to be done. She combed her dark hair, put on lipstick thoughtfully, and surveyed herself in the large mirror of her dressing table. She was about average height, and a little too slender right now, she had been told by her mother on the first day at home. She had been having a whirl during her last weeks at school, and the festivities were relived until all hours in the rooms after lights were supposed to be out. The girls would gather and tell their plans for the summer or recount the evening's activities.

Heather's eyes caught the reflection of Hal Mercer's picture in the mirror from where it stood on the chest of drawers opposite. She went over and picked it up and looked searchingly into the smiling grey eyes. A year ago she thought she'd been in

love with Hal. It had hurt when she learned that
he was already in love with another girl and that he
had only been nice to Heather because of his friend
Marc.

"But you didn't have to kiss me, Hal," she said
to his picture. "You didn't owe that much to Marc,
just because he invited you to come home with him
for a month last summer." The two boys had gone
out on a commercial fishing boat, had boated and
swum in the river, and had spent some time up at
Camp 40. Heather put the photograph back in its
place. She felt no pain.

On second thought, she picked it up and took it
to her brother's door down the hall. He was already
up and out. She went over to his chest and set his
friend's picture on the walnut top. Marc would understand and would never say a word to her about
it. It seemed strange to Heather that Hal had sent
her his photograph for Christmas last year, for he
had become engaged to the other girl only a month
later. She sighed a little. A girl her age had to be
practical about romance, she thought.

She went back to her room, folded the sheet and
light blanket, which one always needed on the
Coast in summer, over the foot of the pretty bed,
and raised the window wide to let the fresh air in.

She stood at the window and looked down.

From here, she could gaze at the distant blue of the Pacific; immediately below her and to the right a short distance, she could see the glassy smooth waters of the Bay. The tall firs across the shore were mirrored in its dark surface, and a little mist was rising from a green cove. She noted that there was a large freighter in the distant harbor, and suddenly she heard the toot of the tug on the river. Picking up her binoculars, she trained them up-river and could see the long barges, fastened to one another by chains, being pulled by Skipper Sneed in his powerful little craft. He had a signal especially for the benefit of the Nicholses who lived at the old Ferry Landing. It made a little musical pattern, and she heard it now, floating out on the clear, still air.

She hadn't been here yesterday when he brought in the tuna for the household, so she conceived the idea of eating a hasty breakfast and driving over to the docks where he would presently tie up his tug. Of course, having relieved it, he could be free; and from long habit, whenever any one of the Nicholses met him, he came home with him or her for a second breakfast.

She hurried down the wide stairs and turned to the service steps leading to the kitchen. Her mother and Marc were in the bright breakfast room having their coffee. The smell of ham and eggs wafted toward her as she came through the hall.

"I just heard the tug! Thought for fun, unless you need me, Moms, that I'd go get Cap'n Sneed and bring him home for a bite of breakfast."

"I know you, Sis. You just want to get a look at all that lovely big barge of lumber, and maybe a sailor or two. It's a Swedish ship, and the boys bane busy," said Marc.

"You! I might have been interested when I was Jan's and Bev's age. But I assure you I'm only interested in the skipper. Do you want to go along, either of you, for the ride?"

"Run along. I'll slow up the next batch of ham, if you come right back."

"Better not, Mom. I'll cook it when we get here." Heather stopped only for a half-cup of black coffee and ran out to the garage, calling back, "I want to get there before he goes to the Chowder Bowl."

She had driven her small car only twice since her return, but it was newly washed and polished, compliments of her brother Sam, who had somehow got up without being called and was off for a day in Portland, too, but not with the twins and their friends.

Heather expertly backed the car out and drove into the highway at the foot of the hill, watching for traffic, before turning into the wide road. The wild rhododendrons were almost gone, but others of June's best native blooms brightened the curves and twinkled in the hedges of willows bordering the Bay. The yellow of Scotch broom was vivid near the town of Bayport, and she saw that the inroads it had made were fantastic. Something should be done about it before it crowded out more desirable plants.

She drove through the waterfront, a *mélange* of fishplants, marine supply shops, fishing docks and commercial ticket windows for the Trade Wind Trollers, famous pleasure boats of the Coast. She could smell the salt water taffy, the caramel corn, and the clinging odor of the sea: the docks and the dolphins with their barnacles. A bevy of small boys was out on the old roadway where the big trucks were now running to empty more huge rocks with which to build new jetties.

It was all so dearly familiar to Heather that she smiled in spite of herself. A few years ago she would probably have been in the forefront of the gang, barelegged feet in old sneakers and wearing a

pair of blue jeans topped by a warm jacket to pro-
tect herself against the wind from the ocean.

The long bridge across the Bay loomed ahead,
and she slowed for the curve. She could see the tug
now, pushing its barges up to the docks. Old Cap'n
would be at his best. With a final toot, his mission
accomplished, he stood by to be cut loose. A few
minutes later he was walking, bowlegged and red-
cheeked, up the gangplank. He had small, twinkling
blue eyes, a reddish beard and scanty hair of the
same shade. He whipped off his captain's hat at
sight of his favorite member of the Nichols family.

"Good morning, Sister!"

"Morning, Cap'n," Heather's voice floated out.
She could recall how embarrassed she had been at
sixteen when he used to greet her with those same
words, for she hadn't wanted anyone to think she
was related to that comic character from the tug.
Shows how much I've developed tolerance. She
walked out to meet him and offered her hand.

"How about going home with me for breakfast?
I came in to get you."

"Good girl! I could do with some food, for I'm
half starved after coming all the way down-river.
Been up since four and ate about five. Thank you,
Sister, for coming after me. Sure have grown up,

and gettin' prettier by the day. Bet the boys around here'll be rushin' you more than ever."

"Flattery'll get you no more ham than usual, Cap'n. My car's over here in the usual parking place."

"Yeah. But in two years, there won't be no more parking places than a rabbit, if I don't miss my guess. Consarn it, Heather girl, are you going to let 'em sell the Nichols plants?" He eyed her belligerently, as though it had already been accomplished.

"No; I don't think so."

"Good! I knew you wouldn't. A chip off the old block. Yessir. Big Bill won't let 'em, 'lessen he's pushed around too much, but he jist ain't got what he used to have since he had pneumony that time. What we need in the Nichols outfit is more guts. And if you ask me, you and young Marc has to be the ones to supply 'em."

"Intestinal fortitude, Grandfather calls it," she said. "Well, whatever its name, Cap'n, don't you worry."

At home she cooked a huge breakfast for the old man, and joined him in consuming it. Sarah was already at work on the tuna, and her mother was sewing in the small room upstairs. Marc had gone downtown to his new office, and the place seemed unusually quiet after she took Captain Sneed back to his tug.

Heather decided to go for a swim. After putting on her bathing suit and a brief robe, she went down to the edge of the river to the small boat which she paddled around the bend to a good pool. It was a familiar place, and she kicked off her beach sandals and dived in. After swimming briskly for twenty minutes or so, she pulled herself up on a raft that she and the twins and Sam had built two years ago. She lay down on it to sun herself, feeling the warmth ooze into her very bones, and grew drowsy.

She was almost asleep when a masculine voice asked, "Anyone home?"

She sat bolt upright and looked into the dark eyes of a smiling young man. She started with surprise. A total stranger, he was possessed of good shoulders and a tapering waist and lean hips, she could see as he pulled himself up on the other side of the raft.

"Hope I didn't frighten you. I'm Seth Barclay." He sat down companionably, and Heather stood up as though about to dive into the water.

"Please don't let me disturb you. I expect you're

one of the Nichols girls. I hear there are three beautiful daughters, and I'll bet you're Heather."

"Yes, I'm Heather Nichols." A plain statement of fact. "Do you live somewhere close by?"

"Not yet. But Dad's hoping to buy the place next to yours."

"Oh, you mean the Weldon place? I heard that it's for sale." She recalled her mother's writing about it last year after a storm had blown down one of the big chimneys. It must be in a sad state, since it had been empty for four or five years, and the dampness on the Coast soon made inroads on buildings.

"Needs a lot of repairs and some additions. Mother's not too happy about it, but it's hard to find a place. Dad's sold on the possibilities. What do you think?"

"Before buying a place, one needs to go over it thoroughly." She hated to tell him that the repairs would need to be extensive. The chimney had been a source of trouble when she was a child and had finally been rebuilt last spring.

She suddenly felt very curious about him. What did his father do, and did Seth work, too? How old was he, and had he gone to college? Restraining herself, she said politely, "I hope you find something to please you. Had you considered building?"

"Not really enough time for that. Dad thought we'd buy this place and get it fixed up in a month or so. Guess we'll stay at the Inn until it's ready for us to move into."

"I really must be going," Heather said. "I've already been out here longer than I intended."

He sprang up. "It's nice to meet you, Miss Nichols. I trust I didn't intrude on you, but it's a little lonesome when you're new in a place. I hope we'll be friends."

She smiled and said, "Bayport's small; we'll probably see each other often."

"As soon as the offices are ready, I'll be working eight hours or so a day. I'm with the Pacific Timber Corporation."

In spite of herself, the smile faded from her lips. Heather felt a chill run up her back. She could think of nothing to say, but forcing herself, managed, "Good luck in your house deal." She dived into the water and, without looking back, swam to her boat. Climbing in, she pushed off. At the very last possible moment before she lost him around the curve, she turned her head. He was standing thoughtfully gazing after her.

CHAPTER 6

The main office building of the Nichols Timber Corporation was the largest, most impressive building in the town. Originally it had consisted of two floors in a square, old-fashioned style of architecture. Soon after the war, when they had continued to prosper, Grandfather Nichols had hired an architect to draw up plans for the modern structure of glass and steel, combined with native timber. On Laurel Drive, parallel to Front Street, it occupied a city block, with neatly landscaped grounds and a shrub-bordered parking lot. A small fountain played its clear stream of water on a park-like flower bed, and white benches and bird baths made an inviting show place for the townspeople to point out with pride.

Parking her car, Heather sat with her mother a moment before going into the building. "There's

Uncle Jon's car; that is, if he's driving the Cadillac he had last fall."

"Yes. He must have got in all right for the meeting. We'd better go in, Heather. Grandpa said for us to get there at two-thirty, you know." Amy looked a little flushed today. She was wearing a pretty dark blue sheer summer suit, with white blouse and hat, blue shoes and purse, her snowy gloves proclaiming the importance of the occasion.

Heather, dressed in a severely cut pale green linen suit, looked very chic and pretty. Her dark hair curled up around the pale straw hat with its circle of flowers, the only utterly feminine accessory she wore. She had tried to look the part of a director. "Really amuses me, you know," Paul had said last evening, "you being one of the directors, Cutie."

"Do you just call me that to deflate me, Paul? If so, save your breath, for I'm going to act the heavy in the cast," she had warned him lightly.

Entering the cool corridor, she walked straight and tall beside her mother. It had only been for the past two years that she had occupied her position, and she could always think back to her first meeting when she'd been too frightened to speak.

The receptionist spoke cordially to them and

told Bill Nichols of their presence by means of the intercom. He came out to greet them, lean of figure, his white hair well brushed and his dark suit faultless. He smiled and took their hands in turn as though he had not seen them at home just last evening.

"Glad you could come a bit early, so we can have a few minutes to visit. No calls, please, Miss Marion," he called back over his shoulder.

His office was furnished with the dark table and desks so well remembered from the old office, but there was a new rug on the floor and a few accessories for added convenience. He motioned them to chairs and picked up his pen. He called for Marc to join them.

Her brother had evidently thought better of his plan to surprise the other Nicholses with the information he had learned, for his grandfather said, "Marc gave me some interesting news today. Seems the Nichols Corporation is in danger of losing a freighter if we don't pay a note I didn't know we owed."

"Tell us more about it, Grandpa," said Amy gently.

Marc came in at that moment. The four discussed the situation until Heather noted the time was at hand to meet with the others in the conference room. Heather and her mother went in alone, and then Marc and his grandfather separately entered the long room with its polished mahogany tables surrounded by ten chairs. The bank president, Mr. Ronald Chafee, was already seated. He was filling his pipe and stood up to shake hands with the others.

"I almost didn't make it, Bill, but I heard it might be important so I canceled another engagement."

"Come now; your golf isn't that necessary."

"Well," Chafee smiled, "it was only a little game." He turned pleasantly to Amy and Heather. "Glad to see the ladies. I would have given up golf gladly. Actually, it was an appointment to speak to a pioneer group on the history of the Bay area."

The others were coming in now: Paul first, followed by his father, a tall, florid man dressed in a light gray flannel suit. He had a stern uncompromising look, and Heather couldn't help feeling that it had been caused by his unhappy marriages: to Sue first, and then later to a widow who had died after four year of marriage.

Jonathon Nichols came, shook hands with Heather and, putting his arm about her shoulders said, "I'm sorry I couldn't be here when you arrived from the East, but business calls sometimes when I'd rather be elsewhere."

"That's quite all right, Uncle Jon. I understood. I'll be here all summer."

"You must come over to the house for dinner soon, and spend the night with Barbara."

"Thanks, I'll do that." She had begun to feel withdrawn from her cousin the last two years. Barbara was older and, even though she'd remained here for college, seemed more sophisticated than Heather felt herself to be. They had few common interests, and Babs held fast to friendships with her college sorority sisters.

The friendly amenities over, the group settled down to the meeting. The other directors were absent. Minutes of the last meeting were read by Paul, and each member was given a small leaflet which summarized the action to be voted on.

Grandfather, as president, rose to speak. Heather recalled that he always did. His authoritative voice rolled out. He came right to the point.

"I believe that we are all familiar with the facts which seem known to most of the citizens of the area; namely, that the Pacific Timber Corporation is buying out many of the other timber and lumber operators in this area. We cannot overlook the fact that some of their recent transactions have been with large, well-established firms; not the little 'gyppo' mills that we thought would be the first to be sold. And now it should come as no surprise to you that Nichols has been approached with an offer to buy the firm. I have discussed this with each of you, not excepting my son Jonathon, who was away when the Pacific firm's agent came to see me. We had a brief talk this morning upon his arrival from Mexico. I suggest that we now have some discussion on the subject." He sat down and looked at his son Jonathon.

"First, I must say that my trip to Mexico City was successful. That mission is accomplished, and we have an order for enough lumber to keep the mills running for at least six months," said Jonathon.

"Why do you say 'at least'?" his father asked.

"Because we might as well face facts. This new concern is bound to sell for cheaper rates. Their production will be tremendous, since they have modern equipment and the latest in transportation.

"They won't be set up for eight months, and you can count on that. Why, their buildings are not going to be started for another month or so. I tell you we have nothing to fear from them immediately."

"Maybe not at the present, Father. But we must look ahead."

"You entertain the thought, then, that we should

consider their offer? I doubt they'd pay us what it's worth to us individually."

"But production costs are up," Paul volunteered.

"Prices are up, too. Compare a thousand board feet of fir today with the price of ten years ago! We don't lack for orders. Our men have kept working, and our schedules have been met. We have orders enough, besides that of the Mexico firm, to run for another year at least." Grandfather had risen again. "I know it's too early for the annual report, Son, but maybe it's time we got a few more things out and took a look at them. Go get the folders from my right hand file, Heather!"

She was gone when the note that Marc had discovered was brought out and laid on the table. Marc, telling her about it later, said that Paul seemed innocent enough about it, but Jon had almost had a "stroke." He had bought the ship against his father's wishes, and had never let the old man know that the corporation had owed a large sum on it for the past three years.

"I want to know if there are other things that have been kept from me?" Bill Nichols' fist struck the table. "Am I considered doddering? Look here, Chafee, did you know about the freighter?"

"I'm afraid I take everything just as it comes to me in the report on the Annual meeting. You know

I can't spend my time going over details. I trust you, Nichols, to keep a straight set of books."

"Now, don't get excited," said Jonathon placatingly. "I knew we could afford the freighter. I've been trying to get Dad to invest in our own shipping facilities for years; it's to our advantage to have the freighter. I planned to give the information to Marc as soon as he'd settled into his office. It's not likely that a boy fresh out of college would have the judgment to pass on such an important item."

"Don't try to mollify me, Jon! I won't have it!" Yet his voice sounded weak and faltering. Grandfather's not very strong, Heather thought.

Amy spoke out of the silence. "Why don't we table the freighter for the moment and take a look at other important items?"

Paul shot a grateful look at her. "Good idea, Aunt Amy. Why don't you tell us how you feel about selling the firm, Grandpa?"

"I'll never sell! Not my share, anyway. That's my final and unchangeable decision. Oh, you can sell your share and the freighter with it, but I'll occupy my office until I'm carried out!" Bill Nichols glared at Jonathon unwaveringly.

"Let's not be hasty, Bill," said Ronald Chafee soothingly. "Now, we're all sensible people. If

Jonathon thought the freighter a good investment, there's no sense getting so upset over it. We can ride along for a time, and not make any decisions until we've had time to consider everything carefully. For my part, I've enjoyed a good income from the shares we hold. I'm authorized to say the same for the port commissioner on the board. We don't want to sell, either, Bill. Well, Fellows, I guess if you'll excuse me, I'll go now. Still time for a game before supper." He rose and bowed to them and left the room briskly.

Just like Ronald Chafee, Heather thought. Doesn't want any part in a Nichols family squabble. Neither do I, she thought.

She rose, too. "Uncle Jon, I think we all need some things clarified. Can we hear just how we stand right now?"

"Certainly." He spoke into the intercom. "Bring in my brief case from my desk, please."

For the next hour the Nichols family listened to his firm voice, in a businesslike manner going patiently over columns of figures. Heather, jotting down some of the information in shorthand, felt confused, and was grateful when her uncle said, "Don't worry about it; I'll have a summary made of all this and sent to each of you. Let's not rush into anything. We can take our time about a decision. After having fifty years of timber in the family, none of us will give it up easily, I can assure you." He became a bit jocose, "Why, what would I do with my time? I'm too young to retire, and too old to learn another trade."

Glancing at him, Heather thought, He looks haggard. This can't be easy on him, either. Her grandfather was pale, and she noticed that his hands were shaking.

"Then let's adjourn," Heather said briskly. "What do you say, Paul and Marc?"

The two young men nodded. Amy smiled wanly. She looked anxiously over at her father-in-law.

"Indeed, yes," she said. "I'd like nothing better right now than a big ice cream soda. Who'll join me?"

Their laughter broke the tension. Marc and Heather jumped up with alacrity. "Come on, Uncle Jon and Paul. Granddad will treat us."

"No, not this time. I've work to do. The rest of you go along, and I'll see you at dinner." Bill Nichols rose slowly. He looked ashen suddenly, and lurched a little. Heather saw him grasp the table with his hands, and she moved swiftly over to his side. He smiled at her and pitched forward before Marc could catch him.

CHAPTER 7

A week later, sitting up in his hospital bed, Grandfather spoke falteringly to Marc and Heather, who had been the first allowed to visit him. Amy and the rest of them had tiptoed quietly to the door of his room from time to time to peep in at him while he was sleeping, but the doctors had forbidden visitors until this afternoon.

Heather's heart lurched when she saw how ashen his face, how thin his long fingers were. He had aged years in a week, and certainly any robustness which she might have fancied he had gained back earlier this month was now gone.

He smiled wanly at them. "Glad you could come, for it gets lonely."

Heather bent and kissed his forehead, and Marc took his near hand. "Don't talk too much, Gramps," he said. "Doc allows us only a few minutes."

"What's going on at the office?"

"Everything's running smoothly, and you're not to fret about any of it."

"Did that order for Stockholm leave the harbor yesterday?"

"Right on time. Good weather and the right tide, and the freighter was loaded on schedule. The bar pilot took it out at five. This morning, we had news she finished loading at Coos Bay and left there on schedule."

Grandfather nodded with satisfaction. "Any more discussion of selling between you and Jonathon?

"Only a little. I'm sitting tight right now until we get the auditor's report for the fiscal year. I think everything can be cleared up financially and we'll start even again."

"Pay off the note?"

"Yes, easily. Profits won't be quite so much, but no one's hurt. I've talked to Chaffee and the others outside the family. Larkin is the only one who thinks it might be wise to sell."

"I'm not one for causing undue worry, but I may not make it this time, Marc. You always want to remember that we've come through the worst times somehow, and in recent years the business has made us quite a nice profit. Don't ever under-estimate the value of the business."

"You can trust me, Gramps. But we're expecting you home in a few days. On my honor! We're all anxious to get you out at the place and baby you properly again."

"The doctor says that you'll be ready to move in a week at the latest, Gramps, if you keep on improving as you have for the past two days." Heather smoothed his arm under the voluminous hospital gown sleeves.

"Any special news from home?"

"Everyone asks about you and leaves messages." She motioned to the bank of beautiful cut flowers ranged on the chest at the end of the room, and the stacks of neat cards and envelopes nearby. "Shall I read a few to you?"

"Thanks, no, I'd rather just visit with you. Nurse is pretty good about reading them to me." He motioned to the adjusting crank at the foot of the bed. "Down a little, Marc?"

His grandson complied with the request, and he and Heather looked at each other anxiously. "Guess I can't stay any longer, Gramps; gotta get back to the salt mines," he said lightly

The faintness of the protest from their grandfather made Heather realize that they'd stayed their limit. She pressed his hand and said, "We'll be back soon. Mother and the twins may drop by tomorrow."

He gave only a slight nod, but his eyes smiled at them.

That was the last time she ever saw him smile. She answered the phone at eight o'clock the next morning. He was in a coma, the doctor said. "There's nothing that can be done; the nurse will call you if there's any change."

For days there was no change for the better. He just gradually weakened.

At Nichols' Ferry everything seemed quiet and subdued. The family had lost its spirit, and though there were callers there seemed to be no life about the place.

One evening Heather went to her favorite swimming place down around the curve in the river and had just pulled herself upon the docks when Seth Barclay appeared.

They spoke to each other, and he climbed up beside her after asking, "May I join you?" He smiled in a friendly manner and said, "I've been watching for you almost every day."

"I've only been here once or twice. Must have missed you."

"We've been busy at the house. We bought it, you know."

"No, I hadn't heard, but then we've had illness in the family."

"How is your grandfather? I hope he's getting along all right." News did travel in Bayport. Of course the paper had carried a brief story of his illness.

She shook her head. "The doctors don't give us much hope now."

"I'm awfully sorry. Is there anything I can do?"

"Thank you, no. There's nothing much anyone can do." She smiled at him. "Tell me about the house. Have you moved in?"

He laughed. "You should see the place! Dad has a crew working almost around the clock. Mother's at the hotel, but Dad and I are sort of camping out in one wing. The painting and papering are almost finished and the new windows are in. Give us another fortnight and we'll be moving in bag and baggage."

"It's been years since I've done more than just pass by and glance in. May I come to see it when you're through?"

"Sure thing! Why don't you come home with me now? As soon as you've finished your swim, that is."

"Okay. I'd like to see what you're doing. The lovely old house seemed so lonely just sitting there all these years. I'm sure it has good possibilities."

He nodded. "Yes, it really was well built, all except that one chimney which must have been added after the main structure was finished. Mother plans to add a family room and a large patio at one side later in the year."

They swam about twenty minutes and then paddled her boat a quarter of a mile below the docks to the beach in front of the big grey house, which stood on a slight incline. The path was ragged and unkept, and new blackberry trailers, salal and moss covered it, providing precarious footing. He forged ahead, now and then stopping and offering his brown hand to her to help her climb the steeper places.

"I'll be doing something about this old path right away. Can't let my feminine friends get torn to shreds coming up this way. Rest?" He motioned to an old mossy stone bench someone had thoughtfully provided earlier in the days. She was panting a little and agreed.

From this vantage point they could see the dark blue of the Bay in the distance and lights, twinkling now on the fishing fleet and other craft in the harbor. The signal light showing the height of the arch of the bridge flashed its red warning monotonously. They were so silent they could hear the echoing bellow of the buoy in the channel.

"Are you cold?" Seth asked solicitously. "The air from the ocean is a bit fresh."

She pulled her white terry robe up closer over her bathing suit but said that she was comfortable. "Maybe we'd better go along, though, if we're to come back down by the trail before dark."

"Let me suggest the long way home, by car. The boat will be all right, won't it?"

She paused a moment, then agreed that it could be left tied up there until later. No one would be needing it, probably. They started up the trail again, and a few minutes later came out into the clearing a short distance from the house.

"Well! I should say someone's certainly been working out here!" She motioned to the great heaps of rubbish, the brush, alders, blackberries, young willows which had only recently overgrown the outer boundaries of the lawns and the old garden plots. "Seems to me there was a large stable over there where some of the children kept Shetland ponies when I was younger."

"Yes, there was and is. Oh, it's badly in need of

repairs. In fact, we may tear it down, except that I'd like to buy a saddle horse and do some riding myself. Dad's not much of an enthusiast, but my mother is. By the way, she'd like you, Miss Nichols. I'd like her to meet you."

"We always like to know our neighbors," she said.

"Good!" They turned a sharp corner and came in view of the house. Lights were on all over the place and she could hear sounds of activity from open windows, smell fresh paint and see the clutter of odds and ends of building materials in heaps at the side of the house.

"Dad's not here this evening. He and Mother drove into Portland early today. When we made the move from the East we didn't ship our older belongings, so they're making some furniture and carpeting selections. Come this way, Madam!" He bowed ceremoniously, and they entered a small vestibule.

The house originally had been of early 1910 vintage, with high ceilings, large rooms and bleak-looking colors, as Heather recalled it. Now the transformation which had taken place was really startling. Big crews must have been at work. Sam had mentioned seeing a lot of activity and the ring of hammers the past week had attested to it. But she had not anticipated all this.

Whole partitions had been ripped out and large windows had been cut out in places where formerly narrow ones had let in only a small amount of light. The huge living room was forty feet long, courtesy of two sitting rooms of the original house. A big plate-glass window looking toward the Bay gave a beautiful view. The old fireplace had been re-furbished and now boasted a beautiful mahogany mantel, and two sides of the room were also done in Honduras paneling, polished and glowing in the overhead lights. One side of the room was papered in white with a gold design, and the other in plain white. New fixtures hung from the ceiling in every room.

Halls were colorful and in good taste. The dining room was newly paneled in birch and the study was in mahogany, with a new fireplace surface and hearth. Brass gleamed from the walls in fixtures and fireplace accessories.

"It's going to be beautiful, Seth!" Heather ex-claimed.

His eyes glowed at the use of his first name and the approval in her voice. "Come on upstairs, please. The paper hangers are almost through with the bedrooms and Mother's quite pleased with them."

There were four large rooms and two baths up-stairs. Soft pastels in two of the rooms, and tones of sandalwood and off-white in Seth's, produced a pleasing effect.

"I was just thinking of the influence of *House Beautiful* and other architectural publications. We've been getting quite home-conscious during the past ten years or so." Heather paused. "My mother would have a field day going through your house. There's nothing she likes better than matching drapery and carpeting and picking the right chair for the right corner."

"Then we must get our two mothers together soon."

An overpowering pang of regret came over Heather. Why couldn't he have been a merchant's son? Or a visiting artist, here for the summer, or a new motel owner? Why did he have to be tied up with the Pacific Timber Corporation? Hateful thought. He was so personable, so likable, that she felt another sudden rush of warmth toward him. It was certainly disconcerting that their newest neighbors, with whom they could have been so friendly under ordinary circumstances, would probably be sworn enemies because of business competition.

"How about a cup of coffee? The instant variety? It goes rather well after a swim. And then you can see what's going on in the kitchen end of the house."

"Thanks, yes. I really could use some coffee."

They went down the back stairs to the big kitchen which was just being completed. Large squares of a light yellow plastic wallboard were being put in place, above ceramic tile of a wedge-wood color. A large stainless steel sink and dishwasher had been installed, and the built-in range and ovens were already in place in brick walls.

"It's incredible. My mother will die of envy!" Heather said lightly. Then she smiled. "No, she won't, really, for she's a darling. She'll be utterly thrilled to find such a kindred spirit for a new neighbor." *Traitor, traitor, traitor!* How can you be so friendly to these people who are only here in Bayport to cut you off from your livelihood!

He boiled water for the coffee, set out some crackers and cheese to go with it, and they sat on two high stools which were at the counter near a future breakfast room.

"Good coffee," she commended him.

"I broil a mean steak at the barbecue grill," he boasted. "Dinner sometime in the future?"

"Yes," she agreed. "It's beginning to get dark. Mother will worry about me and send someone to the docks for me."

"Come along, then; I'll clean this up later."

"Oh, no! Here, I'll rinse them and you set them in the dishwasher as I hand them to you."

A little later she was seated beside him in his sports car, a convertible of bright, dashing red and flashing chromium.

Their road was newly graveled, to be paved later. He swung the car into the highway and within moments was in the Nicholses' drive.

"Heather, I could change and be back to pick you up to go dancing at the Hi-Tide," he said as he pulled up. "I've not had a date in weeks."

"Thanks, Seth. I don't know what to say. We've been pretty quiet lately because of Grandfather. I haven't felt much like doing anything socially."

"But this would be an act of kindness to a neighbor in distress. I'd be ever so grateful. Really, I haven't had a chance to meet anyone anywhere near my age but you."

On impulse, she said, "All right. I'll be ready in half an hour. It's almost nine." He sprang out of the car and opened the door for her.

He smiled into her eyes, and she felt a small shiver of delight run through her.

CHAPTER 8

Amy Nichols came out of the living room as her daughter entered the front hall. Dressed in a pale blue skirt and soft sweater, she looked small and pretty tonight in the overhead light. She said, "I was beginning to worry a bit. You mustn't stay out so long, Heather."

"Pooh! You know that I won't take chances, Mother. The water was fine, but more than that, I went visiting."

"Visiting? Why, who—?"

"The Barclays are fixing that old house up just beautifully. You'll be simply green when you see with what taste and effectiveness they've done it over! You'll be trying to keep up with the Joneses all the rest of your days!"

"I'm sort of pleased with what we have, dear,"

Amy said, looking back into her pretty living room. "And how did you happen to go to the Barclays'?"

"Didn't I tell you I'd met Seth Barclay? He's very good-looking; a little older than Marc, I imagine. I haven't yet learned what school he went to and all that, but I like him, Mother, and so will you."

"Aren't you a bit defensive? Just because he's a Barclay, you don't need to put up fortifications. Of course Grandpa wouldn't approve."

"Is there word from the hospital this evening?"

Amy shook her head. "Poor darling. Do you think I ought to go in again tonight?"

"No, Mother, I don't. Dr. Jack said for us not to come in more than once or twice a day unless he calls us. Come on up with me while I change?" Heather started up the wide stairs toward her room, paused. "Mother, I have a date with Seth; do you think it's all right?"

"Why, of course, dear. Dad Nichols would be the first to want you to go right ahead with your own life. Naturally I want you to go. I'm only sorry that his illness is making your first weeks at home so unhappy, honey."

Heather's eyes filled with tears. "Never think

of me, Moms. It's just losing Granddad that hurts."

They clung together for a moment. "Now, don't cry again, Heather. Go get your shower and I'll get out your dress. What's the occasion? Dancing?" Amy asked.

Heather nodded. She wiped her eyes quickly, went in and bathed them with cold water. "Get out that new pink nylon, won't you? The one with the full skirt, ballet length? Nothing too formal tonight, of course. I'd better wear my white shortie, too, for it's cool."

Her mother watched later while she applied a bit of make-up—merely a quick smoothing on of a light liquid and a whisk of lipstick over her lips. Her arched brows received only a faint tracery of the pencil. Her hair had dried in crisp curls around her forehead. The dress was very becoming, its willowy waist and billowing skirt over a stiff petticoat giving her an ethereal look. She touched the lobes of her ears with her perfume, and added a costume necklace to her slim white throat.

"You look beguiling. Honestly, the fashions are so lovely this year!"

"Thanks to *My Fair Lady*, we're all going feminine again. Truly, Mother, weren't your own dresses this pretty when you were my age?"

"You forget that I was practically a flapper, Heather. Those hipless, short dresses were an outrage! They were so difficult to wear. No whipped cream desserts or fried foods in those days. The chiffons were lovely, though, and I'm glad to see them return. The materials nowadays are so much easier to care for. The new dacrons, nylons and silks are something!"

"And I'm grateful, too. What happened to the twins? Didn't they get home from their trip?"

"No, they called from McMinnville to ask if they can spend the night with one of the girls who is coming down to the Coast tomorrow."

"Portland last week, and again this week! Oh, well, it's really nice to let them go, Moms. Where's Sam this evening?"

"He and Peggy are at a show. They'll meet their gang later; you may even run into them at the Hi-Tide."

"And Marc?"

Her mother laughed. "All accounted for, honey. He's with Paul. They're having a bachelors' conclave, I guess, after their trip together to Salem to see the Governor."

"Come on down with me. I want Seth to meet you," said Heather. "Now, don't bother with your hair. It's just right. Everything about you is just right, Mother, as it always has been."

She hugged her mother's shoulder as they started down the stairs. "I hear his car. Guess I'd better get a scarf, for it's a convertible."

The chimes rang, and she let him in and took him to the living room. Seth was dressed in a light grey suit, and appeared tall and distinguished. He shook hands with Amy and took the chair she offered him. He seemed perfectly at ease, and later Amy confided to her older son that she had been most impressed with him.

They chatted about the town of Bayport and its social activities, and Amy suggested that his mother might like to join her bridge club. He agreed that she would probably be quite interested.

"You must come again," she said in a friendly manner when he and Heather rose to leave.

On their way into town, Seth said, "It's great to find such friendliness in this new place, Heather; I really appreciate it. Sometimes it's rather difficult to make new friends when one has moved around so often. My father has made about five moves since I'm old enough to remember. We just get settled nicely, get acquainted, and bingo! Orders to transfer again. I think it's harder on Mother than on us, though. Kids sometimes make adjustments better than adults."

She agreed with him, thinking how hard it would be for her own mother to pull up the very roots of her existence. She had lived most of her married life here at Nichols' Ferry. Actually, it had been difficult for her to be away her whole term, the first year of college.

"Tell me all about yourself," he said as they neared the first traffic light.

"There's not much to tell. I've always lived at the house except for school in the East. I have one more term before graduation."

"Don't be so brief! Most girls could talk for hours on what you've summed up in a few words."

"I want to hear about you, Seth. You've lived in many places and known many people. Tell me about them."

He drew up beside a large building which had a flashing neon sign, turned off the ignition and said lightly. "My story is going to take a long time to tell—several evenings and a few weekend dates. It's a long account of places and people. But you know, I won't mind in the least telling you all about them, if you'll just patiently wait until later tonight. I promise to tell you only a few incidents each evening."

"Something like the Arabian Nights?"

"Not nearly so fascinating, but I want a long term contract—unwritten, of course, but definitely understood."

"You haven't met any other girls yet. Better not get involved until you see some of the others," she teased him.

He helped her from the car. "I need to look no further, Heather. I guess I know a good thing when I see it."

They were ushered to a corner table in the large room. A small but good orchestra had been hired for the summer to furnish music for the tourists and the Bayport younger set. Several couples were already dancing, but Heather recognized only a few of them.

She and Seth danced, and she found that he was an excellent partner and fun to be with. A thought ran through her mind: I'd really expected to be bored this summer with the lack of social life, but this is not too bad for the first month at home.

About eleven o'clock Barbara and an escort came in. She and Heather greeted each other, and Barbara looked at Seth in surprise when they were introduced.

"I really expected to find you a much older man." She smiled frankly. "My brother Paul has spoken of you several times."

"Oh, yes, Miss Nichols. I recall talking to your brother. And your father, too," Seth said politely.

Heather began to wonder how much of the Nichols business was by now well known to the Barclays. She had never gone back into the office since her grandfather's heart attack, the day of the directors' meeting. She and her brother had not discussed developments much since that day, and she suddenly realized that her interest in her grandfather had caused her to neglect serious consideration of the Pacific Timber Company's offer to buy.

As she danced again with Seth, she wondered if he was being friendly to her so that he could find out more about their business, and then was ashamed that she could have thought his interest in her solely was for that purpose. She danced twice with Barbara's escort, one of the students she had known at the University who was spending a holiday on the Coast. Barbara's friends came and went, seemingly with no serious attachments.

"It's getting late for a working man," she ventured to Seth, as she looked at her watch about twelve-thirty. "Don't you think we'd better call it a night?"

"If you say so, Heather, but not for my sake. I'll probably read for a while after I go to bed."

"Maybe it's time you started telling me your life story," she suggested. After all, we have to begin sometime, if it's going to take as long as you say."

CHAPTER 9

By midsummer the Barclays had moved into their home on the Bay road, and every time she went into town, Heather found herself looking up at the newly renovated place. The old grey shingles had been covered with a new cream-colored siding, with a trim of redwood. The new green roof and shutters enlivened the house, and the walks and the curving drive were outlined by shrubs which continued to grow. The constant care given them added to the attractiveness of the house.

Bill Nichols was still in the hospital when the Pacific Timber Corporation began work on their new buildings at the southern edge of Bayport. Slowly the steel framework began to rise, and reports circulated that the mills' value would be close to forty million dollars, instead of the much smaller sum first mentioned. Bulldozers, giant steam shovels and other heavy equipment worked long hours daily leveling small hills, digging huge ditches and making preparations for the carrying of waste into the Pacific.

A few people met one evening to protest the damage that industrial waste products might cause local fishing concerns, but the resulting weak editorial carried by the press carried little weight.

Sam took a job in the shipping department at the Nichols' mill in late July and came home each evening filled to overflowing with noonday gossip.

"Marc, we're going to lose a lot of our men when the new mills open up," he said one night at dinner.

"What makes you think so?" asked his brother.

"Well, word's out that they can make more money. We probably won't be able to raise wages."

"We'll see. It's a long time until production starts."

Sam nodded. "Of course, I realize that you and Uncle Jon and Paul have figured on all the angles. Gad! It's going really to be something. Did you see the new smokestacks?"

"They'll need 'em to carry off all the smoke," said Jan. "A bunch of the kids were talking at the drug store the other day, and they said if smoke conditions get bad that Bayport will be impossible when we get fogged in from the valley."

"Don't cross bridges, you young fry," said Marc. "After all, Nichols' mills have contributed a lot of smoke in their day, you must remember. People in glass houses—"

"Well, it's bad, but it could get a whole lot worse," said Beverly. "Gee! when you see some of the older cities where there is a lot of manufacturing, it makes you sick to think what could happen to us."

"There's been a lot of progess in smoke control, though. St. Louis and some of the Eastern cities which used to be noted for their smoke problems have installed equipment to take care of it."

"Don't forget the smog of Los Angeles. They haven't licked that yet. Fog makes everything much harder to control," said Sam.

Heather, only half listening, was thinking of the previous evening when she had driven with Seth Barclay to Yachats to the opening of the Salmon Derby. There had been a beautiful moon and dancing in the pavilion outdoors. They had strolled a bit, with Seth's arm about her shoulders.

"What are you thinking about, Sis? You haven't

said half a dozen words since we started to eat," said Sam.

Heather blushed. "It's the good dinner, I presume. I'm half starved."

"Why don't you eat something, then? You're just picking at your food." Jan motioned to the practically untouched serving of baked salmon and au gratin potatoes, the green salad and hot rolls on her sister's plate.

"How was the dance last night?" Bev asked knowingly. "And did the movie stars really come?"

"Of course they did!" There were droves of people from the county there, and lots of tourists and valley-ites."

"Who won the new car?" asked Sam.

"Some gal from Minnesota. Just passing through and stayed over for the opening. She was thrilled, of course, but isn't that just our county people's luck? Cap'n Sneed won a new glass fishing rod, and Sol Porter won the outboard engine."

"Did you have a good time?" persisted Jan. "You and Seth look gorgeous together."

"Yes, we did have a good time. It was pretty late when we got home." She tried to change the subject, for there was nothing so devastating as to be teased by a younger member of the family on

matters of romantic interest. "What's on the agenda
for tomorrow?"

"Would you like to go calling with me?" Amy
asked. She had always kept up the custom taught
her by her mother of repaying calls and making
calls of her own on at least one afternoon each
week.

"I have a swimming date, Mother, but thanks.
What are you twins doing?"

"Barbecue supper at the Hamiltons' at six. Our
gang is going swimming in the moonlight later
then we're going to the late show."

"The salt mines for Marc and me, of course,"
said Sam.

"Wish you'd reserve Friday morning for a conference, Heather. You, too, Mom. Paul and Uncle
Jon have called for a meeting at ten." Marc looked
unusually serious. He added, "I wish Grandpa
could be there, for I think there's something important coming up."

"Like selling out?"

Marc laughed shortly. "You hear too many
rumors, Sam. You kids keep your counsel, and
don't discuss any of our business with anybody.
Hear me?"

"Well, I guess we've got that much sense!" said

Beverly indignantly.

"Well, I should say! What do you think we are, anyway?" added Jan.

"A couple of teen-age cuties." Marc reached over and tweaked Jan's ear, and smiled at her to offset any resentment she might feel. "Of course we know we can depend on you or we'd never let you in on conferences; we're sure you are responsible people, and after all, our dealings will have a big bearing on your future."

Sarah brought in lemon swirl, one of the family's favorite desserts, amid exclamations of approval. Heather, glad of the abrupt interruption, wondered if the family should really discuss business at the dinner table because Sam and the twins were quite young. She could recall how hard it had been to train herself never to discuss the Nicholses' affairs with outsiders.

Grandfather Nichols was barely hanging onto a thin thread of life, and it had become very painful to see him. He had never regained complete consciousness, and it was merely a question of time, the doctor had told them three weeks before.

She reflected that it seemed only natural that Jonathon and Paul should be calling a business meeting of the directors. In all the time she had spent with Seth Barclay, he had not once mentioned the possibility of their selling out to his company. His father would be the consultant of the entire operation and Seth was to be in the production office, as assistant to the manager. He was not quite as young as Heather had thought, she had discovered; he was twenty-five.

Her thoughts kept returning to him through the evening; while the family watched one of their favorite television programs and discussed its merits. It was a rare evening for them; all of them except Grandfather were home together on one of the few such occasions during the summer.

At the meeting the next day, Heather learned that Jonathon had given his word to the Pacific Timber company that they would sell to them. She was shaken when her uncle haltingly admitted it.

Everyone except Paul seemed stunned.

"But why, Uncle Jon?" How did you happen to give your word about something that had never been brought up at a meeting of the board?" Marc rose after a long silence had followed his uncle's words. Jonathon said:

"It came at a time when you were still away. Father had not been at his office for a couple of weeks or so. Paul trusts my judgment implicitly, as the other directors apparently do. I should have contacted Amy, at least. However, there's been no written agreement."

"How far did you go?" Marc asked point-blank.

"A little farther than I care to remember, evidently, since Mr. Barclay was in last Friday to discuss it. He says he is depending on my word, while I thought I made it plain to him that there might only be a possibility. Actually nothing was cut and dried, though if pressed, at the time, I probably would have gone as far as to offer a guarantee. It's too bad that Chafee is away on vacation this week and Grandfather is unable to participate."

Heather paled. It seemed to her that there was a note of relief in her uncle's voice that the other two were not there.

"We can take no action of any kind without the consent of fifty-one percent of the stockholders," intoned Paul.

"True." Jon turned to his son, and in that moment Heather knew that their part in the discussion must surely have been rehearsed, and that Uncle Jonathon had given his word that Nichols would sell to them. Fury surged through her. She fought for self-control for a few minutes, then asked in a surprisingly businesslike tone, "You did give your word, did you not, that Nichols would sell out to the Pacific?"

"Now, now, Heather, let's not get upset."

"And who is upset? I'm only asking for facts that I believe have been too long concealed from the rest of the directors. You and Mr. Barclay had a private understanding, didn't you?" she pressed.

"Really, Cousin Heather," Paul began, "aren't you a little out of line suggesting that my father would do such a thing?"

Marc laughed. The sound was not good. He rose and said quietly, "My sister has the guts to say something that I've been wanting to say for three weeks. We were kept in the dark about the freighter; why, even Big Bill Nichols didn't know about it, and yet he had the idea that there was something furtive going on the day he had his attack. You all know him. A man of iron, ordinarily. He wouldn't have gotten a promise from me not to sell unless he was sure it was going to come to a point where you, Paul, and you, Uncle Jon, were going to insist on it."

"I hope that we can discuss this without getting angry, Marc," his uncle said smoothly. "I assure you that we would be well off to sell out and get completely clear and take our profits and divide them among the stockholders. It's mostly a family affair, and naturally we do hold the controlling interest. Father isn't going to make it. We have had to accept that. Paul isn't as interested in the business as I'd hoped. You all must be fully aware that I'm certainly not getting any younger, and though I dislike to say it, Marc, I don't think you've had experience enough to handle details yet."

"Shall we bring it all out into the open, Uncle Jon?" asked Heather. "What are we offered?"

"There's been no definite offer made. There would need to be a complete inventory of materials, equipment, timber holdings, income, etcetera. It will take weeks to decide on an asking figure."

"That would have to be weighed carefully against the possible income during our entire lifetime," said Marc. "I may not have had your experience, but what I lack there, perhaps I make up for in bulldog endurance and loyalty."

"Hear! Hear!" Paul grinned, somewhat breaking the tension.

"You don't want to kill yourself in harness, Marc. It's a tough job. Your father worked too hard, and your grandfather, too. You could live easily for several years on your profit from the sale.

Maybe you could invest in the new concern."

"No, thanks. I'd worry more about someone else handling my money than I would if I did it myself. Oh, I know that the Pacific Timber has fifty years back of it, but I've not been exactly dead from my ears up all these years. Gramps and I, and Dad, too, talked for hours at a time. Even young Sam knows a lot about the work."

The discussion settled down to hours of details, and Heather noticed that her mother pressed her fingers to her temple now and then. She leaned over and said, "Why don't you go home? Marc and I'll sit it out."

Amy smiled with relief and, making her excuses, left the meeting. Heather began to feel a little fatigued, too, and at about one o'clock suggested that they adjourn for lunch. "Better yet, why don't we sleep on all of this? I'd hate to make any kind of important decision right now."

"The decision must be made by the end of the month, though," Jonathon said. "We've been given a time limit. Pacific has to know, for it means increasing their plants and ordering their equipment. We can't hold them off longer than August."

Going to their car to drive out of town for lunch, Heather said to her brother, "Haven't you known for a long time that this was coming? I've felt it happening; we both knew early in the summer that he wanted to sell."

Marc nodded. "I'm not totally unprepared. My first reaction was that he had no authority to speak for the directors and was certainly unjustified. However, there's one thing I've thought of. We'll discuss it after lunch—just you and I—and then later we can get the others' reaction."

CHAPTER 10

Heather was dressing for an informal supper on the patio when Seth called. She had felt a little more relaxed at home after a cooling tub bath and at first was reluctant to make a change in their original plans to go swimming.

"But I thought maybe you'd like to drive to the Pagan Hut for a swim and dinner there. If we leave within an hour there'll be plenty of time to swim first and then have a good sizzling steak," Seth pleaded.

Heather glanced down at her light summer print, swirling in multitudinous pleats around her bare legs. "May I go as I am? Sun dress, but of course I can add a jacket."

"Please do. Everyone likes to relax there. They have a fair Hawaiian orchestra, and I'll guarantee moonlight." He added as an afterthought, "We really could eat out on the barbecue terrace there; cooking performed as usual by their famous chef."

"Sounds wonderful, Seth. I guess I was a bit tired when the phone rang." Before she thought, she added, "I was at a board meeting until late."

"And what is the feminine sex cooking up for the betterment of the community?"

Heather stiffened. She bit her lip, for she was on the verge of letting him know that she was, after all, a member of a very important directors' group having within their power the decision as to his own future.

"You wouldn't be interested," she said lightly, "though I can think of a number of things to improve the community. However, I'll be happy to settle for the Pagan Hut tonight."

He called for her about half an hour later, and they were off for the ocean highway north of Bayport, bowling along the edge of high cliffs and watching the setting sun reflect its myriad of colors in the water. Past Agate Beach, Otter Crest, Depoe Bay and the Spouting Horns near the Devil's Punch Bowl.

"Does the devil really come at midnight and drink out of it?" he asked.

"Of course he does. And if there are any un-believers about he yanks them up and takes them back to his subterranean home under the ocean. You should see the beautiful marine gardens around here, Seth."

"I'm willing, if a certain guide will show me, say about Sunday afternoon."

"Maybe," she said.

"Do you realize there are only twenty-two days until you leave for the East?" He placed his hand over hers and smiled into her blue eyes.

"Really?" she asked in surprise. "I hadn't counted. The summer is flying fast. So many things to think about and to do." She would mind terribly leaving in September to return to school, she real-ized suddenly. Most of all she had to admit, she was reluctant to say goodby to Seth. It was a bad time to leave, too, because of the situation at the office. What could Marc do without her to back him?

As Seth turned into the wide drive at the Pagan Hut, they saw dozens of cars already in the park-ing area. Walking across the paving to the entrance, they could hear laughter and shouts from the swim-ming pool at the rear.

The large resort apartment-hotel featured its

fabulous main dining room, the Pagan Hut. In colorful redwood, with a full view of the Pacific, it was authentically South Sea Island throughout. The walls were covered with native works and paintings collected by the proprietors on their various travels throughout the islands. Partitions were made of giant bamboo, some of it six feet in diameter, tied together with leather thongs.

Entering, Heather noticed that the brilliant Malayan tiger on one wall seemed to stalk her, no matter where she stood. Friends who patronized the place had warned her that the exotic drinks were works of art and expensive.

They left an order for a barbecued steak dinner to be served at nine, and went to the dressing rooms to change into bathing suits, studying the murals along the walls, native spears, headpieces, shields and colorful floats from fishing fleets. Heather felt almost transported into another world. She had never come to the Hut before, since most of her girlhood friends could not afford the prices.

On their way to the pool, she said, "Seth, I'm going to warn you, I don't go in for their kind of drinks!"

"Someone's been kidding you, honey. One'll taste mighty tempting after you're half frozen!"

He laughed and tipped up her face in the shadows. "Of course, the water's plenty warm; it's the air on the deck that'll cool you."

"We'll see!" she said. She watched him dive from the board and come up laughing. She followed, and they swam a few rounds of the pool before coming up to sit on the edge.

There were by now only a dozen or so people in the water, and they decided most of them were tourists or vacationers from the valley and Portland.

"My grandfather was never certain if he approved of this place for us youngsters," she said, pulling off her swim cap and shaking out her dark curls. "I don't mean the pool. It's of more recent vintage, and it's certainly wonderful with that handsome glass windbreak. Looks like the one at Sun Valley."

"I'll take very good care of you, Heather. Grandfather would admire the steaks we'll get presently. I understand he was a real gourmet."

She regretted the past tense. But she could not very well amend it. "Oh, I mean that the later the hour becomes the more fun everyone seems to have. I hope it doesn't get too uninhibited."

"I'll take you home modestly early," he said

laughingly, putting his arm about her shoulder. "Heather, I'm seeing more of you than I've ever seen of any one girl before. In fact, you're the only one I've ever felt the least bit serious about." He tipped up her chin and looked deep into her eyes. Before she realized his intentions, he had kissed her.

His lips pressed hers very gently; then he drew her closer and kissed her thoroughly. She felt as though she were drowning. She pushed him away a little, and he let her go.

They stared at each other for a long moment.

"I suppose I should say I'm sorry, but I'm not in the least." He took her hand and rose, drawing her to her feet. "There's time for another round; shall we dive in?"

As she toweled her short hair in the dressing room later, Heather felt a surge of mixed emotions. She had been kissed before, by several boys whom she had dated through the years, and twice she thought she might be falling in love. But the feeling had been short-lived. Hal had been the only one of whom she had thought seriously.

Her hands shook a little as she combed her hair and finished dressing. She felt a little cool as the air swept over her on the way to the sundeck where the barbecue pit was now sending out delicious, tantalizing odors of roasting meat.

Seth was already sitting, stretched out comfortably in a lounge chair. Springing to his feet upon seeing her, he moved over to a glider where they could both sit and enjoy watching the bright charcoal embers.

He had ordered a drink for them, and she found that hers was much like a daiquiri. She tasted the small canapés served with the drinks and realized she was ravenously hungry.

"Shall we go in to the dining hall or eat out here?" Seth asked as she sipped the last of her drink. "It's a little cool for you, isn't it?" He had donned a light gray sport jacket over immaculate slacks, but she still wore only her cotton sundress and jacket.

They decided to go in when their steaks were ready to be served. "You must tell me all about your school life," Seth said as they waited. "What's my competition back East?"

"I presume I should look enigmatic, but I'll be honest. I'm not really serious about anyone there. I have dates of course, like most girls, and go to dance weekends at the men's schools and to football games, but it's all just for a good time."

"I can't imagine a pretty girl like you not having dozens of admirers fencing for your honors." He picked up her hand and traced each pretty slender finger. "Have you planned a career? You see, I still know very little about you, for I've been bally-hooing my own achievements, and now I've so little time to find out about your future plans."

She withdrew her hand gently. "There's not been much said about the future. I've tried to talk the office into letting me work this summer, for I'm a fair hand, but I had no takers. Grandpa wanted me to have a real vacation, and so did Mother." She added ruefully, "Just a polite way to let me know they really cannot say much for my ability, I suppose."

"No, I don't agree with you. They believe, like gentlemen of old, that ladies shouldn't work for a living—unless it's absolutely necessary. And of course in your case it isn't.

"How can you be so sure?"

"One hears things in Bayport. The Nicholses are well respected, well-to-do citizens of long standing. Not many other families send their children East to school, give them cars and boats and ponies for birthdays."

"But you've had certain advantages, Seth."

"I'll admit that, for I'm an only child, and my father's always had a good job with an excellent salary. But we're far from wealthy, Heather. We don't scrimp, but neither do we spend like mad. In a way we're quite conservative."

"Would you like to go in now? Your steaks are ready," said the headwaiter.

Seated in a warm corner of the big room, with its muted candlelight, they exclaimed over the food. She ate with appreciation and saw that Seth was enjoying it too. There were huge baked potatoes with whipped butter, garlic bread, and the wooden bowls of green salad with roquefort were gargantuan in size.

The piano and native drums, with a strange string instrument accompaniment, offered them native songs of the South Seas. A dancer with a hula skirt performed with grace; and the audience joined in when asked to sing *Aloha*. One of the guests played the drums with apparent ease, and another one changed places with the pianist. Talk flowed and ebbed and the music provided a tropical background.

"See? It's really quite pleasant," Seth said once when she glanced around appraisingly. "Even Jan and Bev might be perfectly at home."

"I doubt that. Not with their background of beach parties and picnics, rowing and swimming and an occasional dance at the Hi-Tide. Oh, we've led a circumspect life, believe me."

He smiled at her. "I'm glad that was your background, too, Heather, for if there's one thing I don't like, it's pseudo-sophistication. A lot of small town girls have it, you know."

"There's nothing about a small town girl which isn't as good as a city girl," she retorted.

"Don't get me wrong!" he laughed. "The last thing I'd want to do is to get into an argument with you over something we both agree upon."

They finished on a light note, and glancing at her watch, she said, "Cinderella's coach waits without."

"Is it really midnight! It can't be!" He leaned across the table and picked up her hand. "Thanks for coming with me, Heather."

As he settled in the driver's seat a few minutes later, he turned to her and said, "Let's make this a one-night standing date? I mean each week, of course."

CHAPTER 11

Big Bill Nichols passed away early in August, peacefully, perhaps without conscious pain. It was seven when the doctor came by the house to tell the family. Only Amy and Marc were up, but Heather heard the car and, looking down at the drive beneath her window, had a premonition of the import of the doctor's early call.

There was little need for words. Sarah brought coffee in to the living room and everything was suspended for a little while; then a sense of the finality of death struck the household. Callers left cards, the mills closed down the day of the funeral at the large Presbyterian church, and out of respect for such a substantial citizen, many of the business houses closed their doors during the hour.

In lieu of the hundreds of dollars ordinarily

spent for flowers, a large sum was sent to the Heart
Fund, and only family sprays and blankets of white
and red roses filled the altar corner and later covered the grave in the small cemetery just outside
Bayport where Elizabeth Nichols and their older
son rested. Cards and letters expressing sympathy
and regrets continued to come for days, and though
the family tried to keep up with them, it seemed
impossible.

Among the larger contributions to the Heart
Fund was the check of the Barclay family, and
Mrs. Barclay came to the house two weeks after big
Bill's death to repay a call.

By now Heather had begun to get her clothes
in order for the autumn: storing her summer wear,
packing and shipping school clothing. She was
gone the day Mrs. Barclay called, having per-
suaded Barbara to go with her to Portland for two
days of shopping, and to sit in on the College Board
at one of the fashion shops. She enjoyed being with
the other girls from nearby Oregon towns; the
University, the College and many private schools
were represented by others. They modeled the
newest versions of what coeds desired most for
campus wear, evening wear, skiing and other sports
activities.

It was a relief to feel the atmosphere and excitement of pre-college activities again, and she found that she began to anticipate her return East with more pleasure. Yet she realized that she would miss Seth Barclay very much.

They had averaged three or four dates a week since their first date, and the whole summer had been more fun because of the round of picnics, barbecues, swim parties and sports they'd enjoyed both alone and with others. Barbara and her dates occasionally joined them. Marc had not really decided on any particular girl, it seemed, although he had been interested in one or two in summers gone by.

In two weeks she would be catching her plane in Portland, and time seemed to be pressing close on her heels.

She and the other members of the family were called together to hear the reading of her grandfather's will. Although he'd disapproved Jonathon Nichols' attitude and his handling of financial matters, his father had equally divided the remaining share of his stock among the grandchildren, having reserved a portion for Amy and an equal share for Jonathon.

The usual legal matters had to be attended to,

the will probated. The family knew that it would be several months until they would know exactly how matters stood.

"Don't worry about it, Heather. You can bet that I'll phone or wire you if anything needs your vote. You can have it notarized and wired us or telephone, or I can vote for you by proxy, if necessary. I've taken it up with our lawyers here, and it can all be arranged."

"By now I feel that we should certainly keep the business in our family, Marc. Sam and the girls are going to need incomes, as well as you and I. What our father and grandfather worked for, for years, is our due heritage. And besides, I hate to see a big corporation come in and gobble up the Nichols' holdings."

"How would you feel about agreeing to let Uncle Jon sell his share outright to the Pacific Timber people? There could be a division of the property; the Mill 4 plants and the last pulp mill, could be separated without too much disruption. We could probably retain the buildings."

"I feel that Mr. Chafee and the Port Commissioner can give you good advice, Marc. What about the freighter?"

"Let Uncle Jon keep it. He can probably sell it

to Pacific. We could mark it off as a large part of his share of immediate cash, without infringing on any of the operations. Grandfather was right about shipping. I agree that the cost was too prohibitive to buy and keep up the freighter and a crew."

Heather realized how little she knew of details when she tried to read the annual reports. In the end, she left everything up to her brother and to her mother, who knew the timber business best.

One evening she drove to the Bayport area where her family's holdings were situated. Two long wooden plants, a large central planing mill, four smaller buildings which housed paper pulp mills, a narrow gauge railroad which brought in giant logs to dump into the mill ponds, all made an impressive layout. The spicy smell of eternal evergreens permeated the air. The last shift having gone, there were only two or three watchmen around the place; the high steel gates to the enclosure had been locked for the night.

For the first time in weeks, she drove out to the new Pacific Timber Corporation's property. They were making rapid progress, and a night shift was on duty. The grounds were leveled for a mile; huge driveways, already black-topped, wound intricately in and around the buildings which were beginning to loom up with their steel beams. Other cars besides her own had drawn up along the side of the road, showing the interest of the towns-people. Driving past the huge docks which were under construction, she thought of the comparison between the Nicholses' property and this. In the early days, every inch had been earned the hard way. Her own father had worked in the logging camps when he was a young man, just as Marc had done in his late teens.

Her mother hadn't liked Marc staying at Camp Forty. "It's no place for a young boy," she often commented.

"It won't hurt him, Amy. After all, we know how to take care of widow makers in these modern times," Grandfather would say.

"*Widow makers!*" Cruel expression of the woodsmen to describe one of the greatest hazards of the forest: a high branch or huge limb which unexpectedly broke off and crashed down on an unsuspecting victim—not the main part of the tree, which they watched out for.

"Timber-r-r-r!" Sometimes Heather heard the hoarse, warning cry in her dreams, and would run for her life in the narrow confines of a forest glade.

A sudden feeling of homesickness for the sight of

a forest smote her and she drove back through the town and out to the Bay road toward the Barclay place. Would it be forward to ask Seth if he could go picnicking with her tomorrow out to old Camp Forty?

She parked her car in the area designed for guests at his house. As she opened her door to get out, Seth came around the corner of the patio.

"Hello! I thought I recognized that little yellow car. Come in! Gee, this is great!"

"I just had an idea," she said, settling back in the seat as he came across the grass and stood by the car, leaning on the door.

"Hope it includes me." He leaned farther over as though to kiss her, but she said someone would be sure to be looking, so he merely picked up her hand and brushed it with his lips.

"Would I be considered forward to ask you to go on a picnic out to the Siletz area tomorrow to Camp Forty?"

"Let's do! That would be simply perfect. I've been out in the woods only a few times, and I know they're very beautiful out in that region."

"I know a spot that was logged off years ago, cleaned up and reforested. The second growth fir is not big enough yet to cut so it really is just like a park. I'll bring the lunch. Fried chicken, cooked with my own hands."

"If you want me to, I'll barbecue it and you won't have to cook. Don't go to any trouble. In fact, I heard my mother say that if someone didn't eat the gingerbread Kate made last night we'd better freeze it. So I can bring that and some fruit."

"Okay. It's a deal! About ten o'clock suit you?"

She stepped on the starter, but he reached over and turned off the ignition. "Not while I have you in my power. My mother and Dad would be delighted to see you. Please come in and I'll make you a drink." He opened the door firmly. "They're in the solarium watching the sunset and exclaiming over the beauties of Oregon, so you're just in time."

She demurred, but he won her over. She was dressed in a pretty green splashed silk print with a scoop neck and full skirt. She carried a white cashmere sweater and wore white straw pumps. He put his arm about her as they walked across the terrace; in the shadows of the old porch, he drew her near and kissed her.

"I love you, Heather. I love you, darling," he whispered.

Seth! Seth! she wanted to cry out. But she only

smiled at him and took his hand to lead him on into the house.

She had met his parents the first month of their occupancy in the house and answered their friendly greeting. "Seth made me come in! I hope you won't think I'm in the habit of calling on young men," she said, smiling.

Standing, the older Barclay said, "If you were the guest, I should say it would be a very wonderful custom. Do please consider it." He motioned toward the sofa, after taking her hand warmly.

His wife smiled prettily from her small rocking chair. "I'm glad to see you, my dear. I'm wondering if your mother would relinquish the recipe for the wonderful bouillabaisse which Seth told us about."

"Oh, yes, she'd be delighted," said Heather, remembering the old days when her father would don a tall white chef's hat and take over the big bubbling pot in the kitchen, mixing leeks and celery to fry in the olive oil, adding tomatoes, delicate herbs, particularly saffron, and the other ingredients which the sea food recipe called for. "You can get most of the ingredients from Barnacle Bill's up near Depoe Bay," she said. "But you have to watch out for the people who kibitz and eat the spiced prawns before you can add them. In fact, my father learned early to buy a few extra dozen, for the guests liked to sneak them out for appetizers with cocktails."

"You Nicholses know how to live the good life," said Barclay, tamping down tobacco into his pipe. "Seth seems to be quite taken with you all, and when we miss him, we know he's over at Nichols' Ferry."

Seth, returning from the kitchen with a tray of glasses tinkling, said, "We couldn't possibly have picked better neighbors, Heather, and my folks are delighted."

"Thank you for all of us," said Heather, accepting her drink. She looked about the large room, appreciating the deep pile of the beautiful carpet, sandalwood in color, the sheer fortisan drapes, and the clean-cut look of the furnishings. The patio outside had Scandinavian type furnishings of glass and wrought iron, and the bright umbrella above a table lent a colorful note.

Just a few more days and all of this will be a thing of the past for me, she thought. She recalled, too, that Marc had said they might need to sell part of the Nichols' holdings to the Pacific. A wave of bitterness swept over her, but she contained herself and after a while rose to go. After a promise to bring the recipe over soon, she made her adieus and Seth took her back to the car. "I'll see you tomorrow," she said. "Dress for the woods. Blue jeans and plaid, you know." She glanced down at his cream-colored flannels.

"Don't worry!" he said. "I've learned that the hard way, after wrecking a pair of my good trousers early in the summer." He kissed her, and this time she didn't try to withdraw from him.

The shadows had retreated into the dusk, and now darkness was descending. As she drove out into the highway, she saw the bright twinkling lights of the town and heard the night sounds of the beach: an old crane made a loud raucous cry, and one farther down the Bay answered. She rolled her window up, for the air had grown cool and the feel of spray was refreshingly salty. The lights were beginning to spring up at the house, she noted as she turned in her own drive. The twins had company, for she could see cars at the side parking area, and hear laughter as she drew up beside the house. She parked her car in the big garage beyond and walked thoughtfully back to the entrance.

Rock and roll greeted her flinching ears, and she could see the kids down in the big family room, dancing and having fun.

She greeted her mother, sitting in the study by a small fire, reading one of the new magazines.

"Think I should make the kids some popcorn?"

"They'll probably appreciate it. There are about twelve of them down there. Jan was just in a few minutes ago, asking if they could make some hot dogs later, and of course I said yes. Check the coke, will you, honey, and see if there's plenty. There should be another crate or two in the utility room."

"Doesn't the well ever run dry?" Heather said, patting a curl back into place.

"Not when it's been such a difficult summer for the twins, Heather. They've had a lot of fun curtailed. This is their first little party since Gramps' illness, and really, to give them credit, they didn't invite these kids. They just came as a surprise."

Heather laughed. She was thinking of all the times she and Marc had been surprised by kids from town through the years.

CHAPTER 12

As she packed the picnic hamper, Heather felt a twinge of remorse at leaving her mother alone today. There were so few days left. But Amy Nichols had never been one to depend solely on her children for companionship; she had lived a full, rewarding life.

Knowing this was her last year East, Heather was prepared to enjoy it, though she had been tempted several times to enroll for the last year at the University here, so she could spend weekends at home.

"Here's a cherry pie, honey, with Sarah's compliments." Her mother came into the utility room where she was placing the last of the food in the basket.

"Oh, thanks, Mother, but Seth is bringing dessert. Gingerbread, I believe he said." She fastened the lid. "Sure you don't want to come with us? It will be a gorgeous day in the forest and on the river."

"Certainly not! I never go on dates with my daughters!" Amy laughed. "Now I ask you, wouldn't that be something? I'll bet Seth Barclay would toss me out!"

"He's very nice. I'm sure you would be welcome," Heather teased her. "On the other hand, why don't you write out the recipe his mother wants and take it over this afternoon."

"Thus cementing family ties?" Her mother helped carry the basket out to the entry. "How far along is your romance, dear?"

"Not that far, Mums!"

At that moment Seth's car appeared in the drive, and they went out to meet him. Heather was ready. Dressed in gray slacks and a Pendleton jacket, she was the picture of a smart girl going to the country, wearing British tan brogues and a small plaid hat to match the jacket.

The sun was high and the blue of the Pacific seemed dazzling this bright morning. They followed the main road until they came to a cut-off and then turned to the left to cross the bridge over the Siletz River. Presently, leaving the country byway, they came to an old logging road, rough and weed-grown.

"Here's where we hang onto our hats," Seth said.

They clattered and shook as they drove five miles or so on the battered roadbed. The trees began to grow thicker and taller, and the brush reached out tentacles to pluck at the polished sides of the car.

"If you don't want to get it briar-scratched, we'd better park and walk the rest of the way in," Heather suggested. "Look! There's a good place to leave the car." She pointed to a large old spruce tree which stood at the next bend in the road. There was a turn-around ahead, so that they could park without danger of being sideswiped by an unwary driver.

They took the lunch basket and a plaid blanket in its zippered roll and started up a path parallel to the road. Pine needles helped keep it clear of weeds, and they could manage a fair rate of speed. They walked about a mile until they came to the edge of the river. Limpid and cool and green, it looked very inviting. Laying the picnic things down, they sat in the saddle of an old willow root which someone had long ago made into a seat. From here they could look at the pattern of intricate lace woven by sun and shadow through the branches of the low-hanging trees. The rippling water a short distance below them raced to a small waterfall and shallows beyond. Maiden-hair fern and small blue flowers intermingled their beauty, and moss and ivy grew on old stumps and on the river bank, carpeting them with a cushion of tender green.

"It's so quiet you can hear your heart beat," said Seth.

She nodded. "It's almost like a cathedral. Look, Seth, there's a squirrel. Sh! Don't frighten him. Maybe he'll come closer."

The little furry creature stared at them for a moment, then darted away, and a moment later they saw him bridging the stream on a fallen log, pausing to glance back at them from the other side of the river. "Busy gathering nuts, I suppose, for the winter ahead." Seth took one of her hands. "What am I going to do during the long winter, Heather?"

"You'll meet someone else."

"No, really, I'm serious. I can't tell you how much I'll miss you."

"I'll miss you, too, Seth."

"Are you coming home for Christmas?"

"Oh, yes! I wouldn't miss it! I've always come home for the holidays. It wouldn't seem like Christmas without my family and Nichols' Ferry."

"And this year there'll be me. I may not wait, though. If I come to see you, will I be welcome?"

In surprise she asked, "Do you think you might come on business?"

"I assure you it would be solely to see you, Heather." He stood up and took a turn around the improvised seat, striding about as though in deepest thought. "Heather, will you marry me?"

She was so completely taken by surprise that she couldn't answer for a long moment. Then he was at her side, taking her hands within his and leaning over to kiss her. "Say you will, darling. I love you, you know."

"But, Seth, you've known me only a few short months!"

"That's long enough for me to know you're the only girl for me, Heather." He touched her dark, shining hair with his fingertips, lifted her face and sought her eyes.

"I shouldn't hold you to a promise, of course. You're going away, and there's a long winter ahead. But maybe this can be insurance. Look, darling!" He held out a small jeweler's box.

Heather gasped.

He opened the lid, and she saw a lovely diamond, set in a beautiful gold ring.

"Oh, Seth!" She paused. "I don't know what to say. I'm completely surprised. I'd no idea you were this serious!" Tumultuous thoughts were racing through her head. Her mother had taught her to be conservative when it came to marriage. She couldn't possibly become engaged to a man she'd known so short a time. There were so many things to consider. Yet her hands were trembling where she had thrust them into her pockets, and she knew she must give him some kind of answer.

"I understand, Heather. I know it's too soon, but you are going away, and I couldn't help myself. Forgive me, won't you?" He closed the box and dropped it back into his pocket. She wished that he'd not brought it with him on the picnic. He was striding around again, and she looked at his tall, well-built figure, his dark hair, and remembered the depths of his dark eyes. He was almost like the ideal she had created in her youth, different from any of the other young men she had known. Briefly she thought of Hal.

If Hal hadn't hurt me, I probably could accept Seth's proposal, she thought miserably.

"Come now. It's time to start our fire to barbecue the chicken, if the embers are to be just right." Seth took her hand and pulled her to her feet. "Where shall I set up camp?"

She felt a sudden rush of gratitude for his great understanding, and thus entered into the spirit of the occasion as she helped gather wood and build the fire. She joined in preparing the food, and set the plates out on the plaid plastic tablecloth from the hamper.

Seth meticulously turned the chicken on its pivot, and presently tantalizing odors filled the air. She made coffee in a small pot, fire-blackened from many such occasions, tossed salad and placed it on the wooden plates, and heated the rolls snitched from the pantry at home.

"Right from the Waldorf!" she sighed as they began to eat. "It's a luscious barbecue, Seth. Where did you learn to cook this way?"

"At camp, when I was a kid. Used to go to Minnesota to fish with my father when I was in my teens. Once we went to the Lake of the Woods for three weeks. Had a wonderful guide, and he taught me all kinds of camp lore. I can even shoot my dinner and clean it, too, and get an entire meal by myself. Make edible biscuits and fry a mean pancake!" he bragged.

"That's better than I can do," she admitted, "though I have had some Home Ec, and can follow a recipe." She paused in embarrassment. It was as though she were warning him that she wouldn't make him a very good wife, if he expected her to be a housewife.

"There are plenty of other things in life besides being an excellent cook," he said, serving her more chicken.

They lazily finished the meal, and he took the plates down to the river afterward and washed them in the shallow stream near the waterfall. She gathered some of the ferns for her mother's rock garden and packed them in cool wet moss so that they would keep until they got back home. Later, they walked on down the road to Camp Forty, and she visited a few minutes with the camp cook.

"It's not like the old days when I was a kid," she said when they were returning to their car. "Nowadays everyone has a car and they drive into town to see a movie, or go into Bayport to dance. People out here used to get so lonely that they'd do anything for entertainment, including spelling bees and baseball games."

As they were driving back through the forest over the logging road, she said, "It's been a lovely picnic, Seth. I'll always remember how cool the woods were, and how pretty the moss was on those old rocks. And not the least of all, how good the chicken tasted."

"Good enough. And I'll remember how pretty you looked all day, and how much I'd like to kiss you." He kept his eyes on the road. "If at Christmas time you haven't found someone you like better, Heather, may I ask you again to marry me? You'll find I'm fairly persistent."

She put her hand on his on the steering wheel, and his fingers immediately curled up over hers.

"Yes, you may, Seth. And I do want you to know that there's a very good chance that I'll say 'Yes' at that time. I do like you very much, Seth, so very, very much."

He pulled her to him and kissed her for a long moment.

CHAPTER 13

Late in November, her brother wrote her that the final negotiations between their Uncle Jonathon and the Pacific Timber Corporation had been completed. One half of the Nichols' holdings had been included in the sale which they had finally agreed upon.

"Much to my surprise, Uncle Jon has gone to work for them," Marc wrote. "He doesn't have the responsibility he did when working for himself, I presume, although his hours are almost as long. He confided in me, in a harassed manner, that he didn't feel up to looking for another job and he's still young to retire. Actually, Heather, I think we shouldn't be too hard on him, for he seemed lost the first week or so. I tried to get him to take a trip, but he declined, saying that he'd traveled enough to last him a lifetime."

Heather, reading the letter carefully a second time, realized that they faced trying times ahead. Paul was still in his office, as an executive, for which he was being well paid. She was amazed he hadn't immediately left Bayport, for his interests were varied, and she was convinced he wouldn't stay with them long.

By Christmas when she had arrived at Bayport for the holidays, the new mills were going into limited production. As they drove into the town, after Amy and Marc had met her plane at Portland, she saw steady black columns of smoke above the vicinity of the Pacific Mills.

"See our beautiful smog! L.A. has nothing on us," said Amy. "I'm just sick about it, for of course we get part of the blame, too. But look at the contrast. Little old Nichols is just about one fourth as large."

With dismay, Heather noted the thinner column above their plants. Last year at this time, they, too, had been in full production and all the mills were running. Now one half the production had been curtailed so that they seemed almost idle in comparison.

Marc avoided going near either of the mills and changed the subject. They had touched only lightly on it on their way from the airport. Heather realized from the strain on her brother's face that pressures were beginning to build higher in their offices.

She felt impatient to see Seth, although she had written him that her family would meet her as usual when he had asked if he might. She had begun to realize that her resentment against the rival firm transferred itself to Seth; sometimes she discovered she was thinking of all the Pacific personnel with bitterness, including Seth and his father. It startled her and made her think how unreasonable one could become when there was rivalry between business firms.

However, she reminded herself, they had agreed to the sale of part of their holdings, and though she had bitterly opposed it in the beginning, they could not hold it against the Pacific people. More and more of their men had gone over to the new mills even before the sale, and the pay scale, she was sure, had something to do with it. Marc, as the new president of the Nichols Company, had managed to put through a raise for their crews in all departments.

A number of things contributed to the loss of their men to the rival firm. An accident in the chipper, in which one of their older employees was fatally injured, caused a turnover. The safety regulations were reviewed and new equipment took the place of some of the old, so that the expenses for the year had increased tremendously.

Because the new plants were putting in an excellent pump line carrying wastes far out into the ocean, the Nichols plant had to rebuild its own.

Later during her visit, Marc said, "I'd no idea how run down some of our equipment was. Much of it was worn out and needed replacing anyway; having had a chance to look over the new mills, I can see why Uncle Jon wanted to sell to them. Those big modern saws cost a fortune, and the huge vats for the pulp, and the installation costs are terrific; but they'll make a fortune, too."

"Couldn't you get Uncle Jon to come back here?" she asked at the office one afternoon when she and Marc were going over figures.

Marc shook his head. "He's been good enough to discuss some of our problems on his own time. What's more, I don't blame him. He really has a much easier job than we could afford to give him. To come back to the production headaches here would just about finish him."

She suggested hiring a new production manager, and Marc agreed to investigate the possibilities.

"That would help a lot, Sis. We'll see what can be done."

Heather entered into the festivities of the holidays at home, helping to trim the tree, with assistance from the twins and Sam and of course, Seth, who came over to her house almost every day.

It was the custom in the family to set up the tree and trim it on Christmas Eve, then to have a midnight supper of oyster stew and hot breads, newly baked. Earlier in the afternoon Heather and the twins had gotten the boxes of familiar trimmings out of the attic. Marc and Sam cut the tree that morning, a lovely little spruce from one of their own hillsides. Several strings of new lights shimmered from the big outdoor trees which stood like sentinels on either side of the patio, where their father had planted them long ago in anticipation of Christmases to come. All through their festivities, they kept remembering other holidays when the family had all been together.

Seth arrived at eight, handsome and merry, his arms laden with gift packages. The twins wanted to go to work early, for they were going caroling at nine with a group from their church.

Heather, dressed in a bright red flannel dirndl and a white silk shirt, looked like a pretty Christmas ball herself, Sam said. He draped a rope of silver tinsel about her shoulders and said, "I proclaim you the spirit of Christmas Present!"

"Queen of the Yule!" added Seth, picking her up bodily and seating her on the top of the stepladder which he had just set up, so he could go to work. The spun glass angel was ready to be placed on the topmost branch of the tree, and the glitter and shimmer of many trimmings littered the deep pile of the carpet.

"Please let me down! I'm holding up operations!" Hateful word! Why had she used it? It only made her think of the mills.

Seth lifted her down and kissed her soundly under the mistletoe above the door, to the glee of the twins.

"You've been conniving with Seth!" their sister accused them.

"On the contrary, I put it there myself yesterday afternoon when I was waiting for you to come down," said Seth. Then he whispered, "Do I have to depend on mistletoe?"

She kissed him deliberately and said, "Only cowards and kids without finesse depend on mistletoe."

At nine the tree was finished.

"I'm glad we keep it old-fashioned at our house. Oh, we've tried the all white and the all blue trees a few times, and the girls have them upstairs in their rooms this year, but I go for the quaint old customs," Heather said to Seth as they stood back and admired their handiwork.

"Me, too." He took a step toward the tree and said, "I think this silver turtle dove needs to be closer to those pears!" and made the slight change.

Two station wagons of teen-agers pulled up in the drive and spilled out their carolers, who lined up on the patio and sang "Deck the Halls With Boughs of Holly" and "I'm Dreaming Of A White Christmas."

Fortified by hot chocolate and their numbers strengthened by Janet and Beverly, they presently continued into town to make the rounds in places formerly decided upon.

Amy, who had been upstairs wrapping packages for the Children's Home, joined Seth and Heather, and Marc, who had been late getting home for dinner, came into the festive room. The fir logs were burning brightly in the big fireplace, the lamps were dimmed, and the bright lights of the tree added their brilliance to the occasion.

The two men greeted each other in a friendly

manner, and Marc offered Seth a cigarette. They talked about the weather, about Christmas, and how nice it was that Heather could be home for a fortnight.

It was a gay evening, and gayer days followed, and Heather realized that no serious discussion of business had taken place between her and Seth. He drove her back to Portland to catch her plane on New Year's Day.

"There was one place I meant to take you, Heather. I realized you've never seen my office, and I'm sorta pleased with it, you know."

"I've never been in the Pacific grounds," she said.

"Why not? Practically everyone else in the community has gone through the entire works. Gee! I could have taken you. I wish I'd thought of it."

"I'm not particularly anxious to see it," she said. "After all, a firm that is giving us plenty of headaches is not exactly—" She broke off, biting her lip.

"Heather!"

"I'm sorry, Seth. I didn't mean to say such a thing. It just slipped out. You're not to blame, of course." Bitterness crept into her voice and she turned her face away from him.

One of his hands left the wheel and reached for hers. "Darling, I'm sorry. I had no idea you felt like this. You've never let me know. I hadn't even guessed that it was troubling you." He whistled. "Say, for someone as closely associated with it all as I've been, I must say I've been terribly dumb about it."

"How could you help knowing? You know about our men leaving to go to work for your company, and about all our new equipment and poor Marc's problems, didn't you?"

Caution was in his voice. "But you sold about half of your mills to Pacific. Naturally, the men would want to go with their work, Heather. Come now; don't be worrying your pretty head about such things."

"I suppose you're one of those old-fashioned men who think women know nothing of business matters."

"No, of course not! Women are smart creatures. Statistics prove that they do most of the buying in our country, and own about three fourths of the money. *Never underestimate the power of a woman,*" he said lightly.

"You make me furious!" she said.

"Oh, come, Heather, I'm really sorry. I didn't

realize you knew so much about the business end. Of course I have heard that you're one of the directors, but I supposed that it was only an honorary position."

"I vote and share problems with the others," she said in clipped words.

"You're angry with me, Heather, and I think that's a bit unfair. I only happen to work for the other firm. I'm not your enemy, darling. I'm—" he broke off—"confused, right now. Darling, I wouldn't hurt you or your family for anything, don't you know that? You mean more to me than all of the Pacific Timber Corporation's vast resources."

She said contritely, "I'm sorry, too, Seth. It was really rude of me to accuse you unjustly of having anything to do with our problems."

"I've been buried in my work, Heather. It's been stupid on my part not to see your problems building up. They may get worse, you know."

"How can they?" she cried. "Oh, Seth, how can you be any part of a huge concern that comes in and deliberately gobbles up the poor independent organizations which have helped to build our country out here?"

"That's progress, Heather. It's not my will or

any one person's will; big business has a way of sweeping up the little businesses in its path. Oh, there's no reason why the Nichols Corporation can't go right on making a comfortable income for your family, Heather. I understand that your immediate family are now the sole owners?"

"I think you know a lot about the Nichols holdings that could come from only one source of information." She was thinking of her uncle Jon's connection with the rival firm.

"Bayport is a small place, Heather, and news travels fast, even though some of it may be false."

"If you think my family is going to see your company ruin us, you're mistaken," she said, bursting into tears.

Seth pulled the car off the highway and stopped. He turned to her, but she was wiping her eyes and saying, "Go ahead. I'm sorry. Only one more indication of the weakness of the sex, of course. You've scored several good hits this afternoon."

Grimly he started the car. He drove in silence for several miles, then said, "I wish I could tell you how sorry I am, Heather. And for this to happen on our last afternoon together makes it doubly bad." She could read his thoughts. He had planned to say many things to her on this drive, and now he might never say them.

It was too late. She had shown him how unreasonable a woman could be. She wished she could say something to change the situation, but words would not come readily to her lips, and she sat in silence until they came to the airport. Her big plane was already warming up its engine, and she had to check in her luggage.

CHAPTER 14

Their first letters after the holidays were restrained, and it was weeks after the trip to the airport before they got back on the old easy footing.

In early April Seth flew to New York, and she met his plane. She found herself trembling as the passengers streamed through the gate and she saw his eager look, the quick smile and the wave of his hand. Then he was kissing her and she felt a surge of happiness sweep through her, washing out the old, painful bitterness.

They had a wonderful visit. He took her back to the campus and stayed at a nearby inn. She proudly introduced him to her friends and was the envy of all the girls who met him. They attended a dance, and he sent her a lovely corsage, and it seemed right and wonderful to be receiving these attentions from him.

"He's a very eligible-appearing man," her roommate said at one o'clock after a Saturday evening. "Tell me all about him. How come you've been keeping him a secret?"

"Not really. But it's a long way to Oregon."

"Are you going to marry him?" Peggy Allen came right to the point. "For if you aren't, I think there are two or three others around here who might try for him."

Heather smiled. She took off her white glove. "See?" The diamond that Seth had first produced on their picnic, so long ago in the Siletz forest, now rested on her engagement finger.

"That's just like you, Heather Nichols!" Peg squealed. "You know, you're perfectly maddening. Most of the rest of us would have wakened everyone on the floor and showed it off." She squeezed Heather's shoulder. "Isn't it romantic? Just six more weeks of school, and now you're engaged. When will you marry?"

"Not for years yet," said Heather.

"Why?"

"Oh, we need to have financial security so that he won't have to worry too much. He's very considerate, and wants to build me a house."

"Not many men want everything ready to hand their brides on a silver platter." Peg began to brush her hair. "Do you really believe in long engagements?"

They laughed. They'd discussed almost every subject during these years they'd roomed together. "It's too late to start that again!" said Heather.

"You mean you can sleep?"

"At least I can pretend to be dreaming," Heather amended.

On his last day they went to church in the morning, and he meekly agreed to make a few calls on some of her favorite teachers. In the late afternoon they drove out into the country for a picnic supper, and he took back with him the picture of a flower-pretty meadow and a girl in a flower-printed dress on a beautiful April day.

The last few weeks of her Senior year were filled with pre-commencement and commencement activities. Her mother and the twins flew East for the big event, but her brothers and Seth were unable to attend. All the farewells, the promises and the final arrangements about future meetings had been made, and Heather's spirits began to droop a little. She found it difficult to say goodby after four years, especially to Peggy, who was leaving immediately to spend the summer touring Europe.

"Come with me," Peg said at the last moment. "Please!"

"I can't this time," Heather said. "Maybe another time. Let me know when you go again."

"Don't you dare marry Seth until I can be there to be bridesmaid. Remember, you promised!"

On the plane going back to Oregon with her mother and the twins, Heather began to feel the letdown. She was very tired, for the past few days had been hectic. It felt good just to sit back and close her eyes and pretend to sleep. Janet and Beverly were impressed with their first long flight and enjoyed every moment.

On the trip home, Heather learned that the girls were going to attend the University next fall, and she tried to find out if that was through their own choice, or through financial necessity.

By the time the plane reached Portland, she felt that she had a rather clear picture of the family's situation. Marc hadn't written to her very often since January, and she had not been able to translate the cold figures of the semi-annual report of the Nichols' operations completely. Her mother, however, was able to fill in the gaps.

"We're on a rather precarious footing at the

present time. Usually we have been able to put some of the profit back into the business, but this year there's been little ready cash, since we've sold half of the holdings. Naturally we've had to borrow money to install some of the new equipment and hire the new production manager. Marc is very pleased with Mr. Holloway, however, and he will prove his worth to us, I'm sure. By careful handling, we'll be ahead this time next year. But right now we have to retrench, Marc says."

Hateful word. Her grandfather used to use it. Oh, it had a familiar ring to her, but in earlier days it hadn't meant so much. "I'll help out in the office," she said, "if there's a place for me."

"Probably the girls will be taking their summer vacations as usual and you could substitute."

It turned out to be more than that, she learned when they arrived, for one of the older employees was getting married and leaving for California with her husband, who was stationed in one of the Air Force bases. So she became a full-time employee of her own company.

Seth had left a message for her to call when she arrived at Nichols' Ferry. He joined them for dinner and they went out for a ride later. On this, her first night at home, she felt their old time companionship and was happy to see how eagerly he greeted her. All through dinner, she could still feel the warmth of his kiss and his hard arms about her.

There was a large silvery moon riding high above the ocean, tipping the waves with light. Leaving the town behind them, they bowled along the edge of the Pacific, following the curves of the new highway, climbing the steep hills and slowing down for the mist-filled valleys.

"It's wonderful to have my girl back home," said Seth, smiling at her and putting his hand over hers, driving with his left. "I can't tell you how much I missed you and how long these last weeks of school seemed."

"I was anxious to get back home."

"Heather, I've found a pretty house I'd like you to see. I think I could manage to buy it for us, if you like it."

Her heart almost stopped beating. A house? That would mean marriage this summer probably. She felt breathless. He was waiting, and she had to say something, she didn't know exactly what to say. The words, "Where is it, Seth? were almost inaudible.

"Near the bridge, high on a bluff, overlooking

the Bay. Opposite the park; I think you might like the view. It was built of stone a few years ago, and I think it's in excellent condition."

But you can't set a date for a marriage just because you've found a house you like, her heart cried. She felt a little trapped. She hadn't thought about it being so soon.

"I thought I'd help in the office this summer, Seth."

He removed his hand from hers. Perhaps it was because of the sharp turn, but maybe it was because of discouragement.

"Marc needs me, and I've already promised him I'd help out," she added.

"I see." He kept his eyes on the ribbon of moonlight ahead. "It's been such a lonely winter, Heather. I was hoping that you'd want to set the date for this summer."

She was silently thinking. She hadn't been ready for this. A little shiver went through her. Why was she so uncertain?

"Seth, I must talk to you, I simply must!" she said in a low voice.

"Why, of course, darling. What is it?"

"I don't know how to say this, but I'm afraid of what the timber companies are doing to us. To you and me, I mean."

"What on earth, Heather? The two have no connection," he exclaimed. He slowed the car, turned out into a wide parking area near picnic benches, facing the ocean. They sat watching the breakers on the moonlit beach below. "What can I say, Heather, to help you understand that your family's business and my work should never enter the picture?"

"But can't you see that they do?" She began to cry. "Your company has practically forced us out. Oh, we thought everything would be all right, that we could manage, even after we sold part of it to you. But I find upon my arrival home that my brother's under a severe strain. Mother indicates that we've had to go heavily into debt and, frankly, I'm a little frightened."

He turned to her and took her in his arms, and she clung to him. "There, there, don't cry, Heather. None of it's worth your tears. I hate to see you so worried. I could look after you better if we were married. Is there anything that I can do?"

"No. I think the new manager will help us a lot. But can't you see, Seth, that right now is a bad time to talk about getting married?"

"But it might be the end of your troubles. I don't

make a big salary, but it's adequate for us; we could live modestly well on it."

"It's not just that. It would be letting Marc and the others down." She wiped her eyes and sat up rigidly.

"Heather, why don't you get Marc to sell out completely? I honestly believe that it would be the best thing for you."

"How can you possibly say that unless you know all the circumstances?"

"You've just said that your family has had to go into debt heavily in order to buy equipment. I know the price of modern installations, and I know that you've had to add some very expensive machinery to your plants. News gets around in Bayport."

"Yes, indeed it does. Enough so that the twins know some of the things that are being said. For instance that it's just a matter of a few months until Pacific will take over our whole operation!" she said angrily.

"You must not listen to such rumors. Little people gossip over nothing. Don't pay attention to anything like that, Heather. My father is a very ethical man and would never do anything underhanded, as you should know by now."

"He would not think of squeezing the Nicholses out?"

"Certainly not! He has nothing to do with the price of your new equipment. Even a girl ought to know that!"

Anger quivered between them. Their voices were hoarse, and she was trembling again. She hadn't meant to accuse his father of underhanded methods.

"I think it's quite possible for two rival companies to work side by side amiably and possibly to each others advantage," Seth continued.

She felt a sudden pang of shame. "I have acted like a very young, inexperienced kid, Seth. Ideally, we could work together, of course. But who's going to take the blame for all that's being said? I mean the smoke problem, the overload on the schools, and the juvenile delinquency that has suddenly struck the town and this area?"

"There are many problems in a boom town that have to be solved. As far as blame is concerned, let's not you and I speak of blame. Responsibility for the smoke is something that Pacific must work out. Nichols' smoke problem is very small compared to ours. We have our engineers working on a solution and I hope that they will find it soon, before some of the newer buildings become blackened."

"I even heard that the school budget hadn't been passed!" she said indignantly.

"That isn't exactly Pacific Timber's fault, is it?"

Even as the torrent of words poured out, she knew that mere talking wouldn't solve the problem. The new mills had brought hundreds of employees into the area, overcrowding the buildings, overworking the teachers and creating a housing shortage.

"We have to educate the people as to their needs. It isn't that they vote down the schools; it's that many of the people who need the buildings for their children, they don't go and vote at all. They passed the bonds on the second go-round, having failed the first time; then when they came to the annual budget election, many of them thought every thing was taken care of and failed to go to the polls."

She was surprised at his knowledge of school affairs. "My mother has served on school boards in almost every town we've ever lived in." he explained. "The people are going to have to pull together to take care of their local problems. With more state money available now, they will not be taxed as much as they might have been without the state aid. Of course, if you get a few disgruntled politicians working against anything and claiming it will hit the people's purses, you're bound to get negative votes, too." Usually, he went on to say, it was the people who were angry at the world anyway, the rabble rousers, the unthinking or selfish who, not having children in school, did not care about education.

She was further amazed that he knew so much about the school situation in general, and the area in particular.

"Why not? My folks were badly shocked when they heard the budget wasn't adopted. Many new-comers are loath to stay in an area which votes down its school budget; and they're bound to lose their teachers and fail to hire new ones, because teachers don't have to hunt for jobs any more with other states begging for them."

How did we get into this discussion? she was thinking. Yet she was pleased that Seth cared enough about the community to be outraged at the recent "disgrace" to the area.

"People will have to get out and really work for what they want in the way of progress. The old die-hards and 'Let George Do It' types are always ready to let someone else bear the burden."

"You sound like a good Mayoralty possibility," Heather suddenly giggled. "Or the next Governor!"

"Let's just say that I take my civic responsibilities seriously," he answered. He put his arms around her. "Not mad at me anymore, darling?" he whispered.

She shook her head. He kissed her and she returned the kiss, her heart beating very hard. *I must never let myself get angry again over anything that he cannot help.*

But they didn't continue the discussion of marriage and did not set a date.

CHAPTER 15

By August the new Pacific Timber Company's huge mills were in full production. The whole area around the Bay was like a community of busy ants, Heather often thought, as she watched the ever-growing line of cars waiting at the gates at the close of the day shift, or the opening of the morning shift. Traffic problems had quadrupled in six months, and several accidents had occurred on the winding narrow roads surrounding the region.

When the temperature rose in the valley across the Coast Range, the fog thickly blanketed the country around the Pacific and the Bay, and the holiday visitors, attempting to escape the valley heat, added that much more traffic confusion. The heavy columns of smoke rising from the mills combined with the fog to make the hated "smog" known to citrus-growing regions in other parts of the country.

"It's a lot worse," panted the perspiring Mayor at a citizens' meeting in mid-August. "Why, the laboratory tests show that the percentage of poison in this smog is enough to kill us if allowed to continue for some time. Look at London and the high death rate when they get this same kind of combination."

Discussions not only at this meeting, but also at women's civic organizations, brought forth other complaints. The new church was beginning to show the ravages of the black brush strokes of the fog which persistently covered the town throughout most of the day. Harassed housewives complained that their washing streaked on the lines outdoors, and that their windows became thickly coated with a grey, oily solution which defeated them.

At the enrollment of students prior to the opening of the schools, it was found that double shifts were to be adopted, and the parents called an emergency meeting to protest.

Amy attended the meeting and was most unhappy at the prospect for the coming year. Reporting to Heather and Marc at the dinner table, she said, "Why, the very walls will be splitting. Think of the poor teachers! Even with the double shifts, there will be about forty pupils to a room in some of the grades. One room was to have fifty, but I stood up and objected."

"Good for you, Mother," said Marc. "I can't imagine more than thirty students in a room which has been built to accommodate twenty-five in the first place. Now, I ask you, where was that room of fifty supposed to be taught?"

"On the stage at the Horace Mann Building."

"Not really!" exclaimed Heather. "Then what becomes of the P.E. period? Where does the gym teacher take the kids on rainy days when they can't be outdoors? Which, of course, is a large number of days throughout the school year here on the Coast. It's impossible!"

"Well, they've rented church rooms and empty buildings, although they've had to pay a high price for them because commercial occupancy would net the owners real profit. But here's the problem. The Superintendent says it will probably be impossible to find enough teachers. State shortages do not help our situation. Now, I ask you, why should a teacher want to take a position in a community where the budget election had to be held twice?

Isn't it enough to teach without worrying if you're going to have supplies and rooms to teach in?"

"Mom, is it true there'd be only about two months of school if the budget didn't go through?"

"Quite true! A lot of thoughtless people said they'd have school anyway. How could they? Teachers are people. They have to eat, and have a place to live like other human beings; therefore the salaries contracted for would have to be paid, whether they taught or not. That would leave very little to keep up buildings, and buy supplies and textbooks for the year. This unit system is big business which involves a great deal of money. You don't build a modern building today for a song. We need forty more classrooms in the unit today. Remember, Heather, when Barbara was graduated from high school, there were only twenty people in her class? Actually, there were less than one hundred in the total enrollment that year."

"I remember," said Heather.

"Gosh!" exclaimed Sam, "there were four hundred kids in Senior High last year, without the new enrollments this spring, when production at the mills picked up forty percent. I remember there were thirty-five kids in my English class, and one of them had forty!"

"Do they have enough teachers for the double shifts?" asked Marc.

"Not yet. Mr. Mack is scouring the agencies, the colleges and Universities and the community agencies. One woman in our group this afternoon volunteered to see if she can be certified. She taught before marriage, but that was twenty years ago. She is a college graduate, but she's not sure about certification requirements for Oregon."

"Gosh! Sis, why don't you teach?" asked Janet.

"Because I'm not prepared to teach. Just being a college graduate doesn't make one a teacher. You have to take specialized training in practice teaching, psychology, and education generally. Oh, no! Not I! Teaching's a profession which requires patience and real dedication. Imagine being responsible for teaching a child to read! You can make or break a child in the classroom as far as his wanting to be educated is concerned."

"Much of that is predetermined at home," said her mother.

The long discussion which followed showed how serious the situation at Bayport had grown. The schools drew from an area of several miles beyond the town, and children were brought in by buses.

The schools opened with a shortage of five teachers. And by overcrowding classrooms again, making an almost intolerable load for some of the rooms, they were able to start the term.

The twins left for the University for Rush Week, which was the fourth week of August. Sam was planning to attend State College and had waited until the last week to go.

Each of them had been provided with a trust fund set up by their grandfather, at birth, to insure their educations. Heather began to realize how much it had been padded by her own parents' supplementary money so that she could attend the expensive college of her choice.

Even though her salary was not very large, she was determined to help see the girls through college if it came to that. When her grandfather had taken out the endowment policies, schooling had not been nearly so expensive. World War II and the Korean War, increased labor costs and rising prices had made enrollment fees and board and room prohibitive for average high school graduates from families of modest incomes.

Heather brooded about some of the twins' friends who would have liked to go on to college, and who could have done well academically, but because of finances, could not attend.

"It doesn't seem right, Seth," she said one evening. "Think of all the money it takes to test one atomic bomb. Just think how many of our young people it would put through college!"

"Just hope and pray that some day we won't have to use that atomic bomb," observed Seth. "Actually, it may be a preventive measure to carry on a testing program."

Thinking back to some of her classes, she recalled some of the heated discussions in History and Social Science.

"I realize how protected I've always been," she said. "We did feel the war rather keenly here on the West Coast in the last two years of World War II, but I was too young then to know much about it. I remember the blackout curtains we had to use at the house; and years afterwards, I heard about the submarine and its crew that was captured just off our Coast." She shivered, recalling the tale of an older woman who had owned a motel on the beach at the very place where the night action had taken place. "It was kept very quiet by the older, responsible people of this area, but I know we weren't allowed even to swim any place except right in front of our homes, here in the Bay. Cape

Perpetua and the other hills were out of bounds, and the fishing fleet was carefully searched in and out of the harbor."

"America has been very fortunate, Heather. I saw only a little of the Korean action, but that was enough to make me keenly aware of the need for caution and preparedness." He had never discussed the service he had seen, and after a few attempts to draw him she had not gone farther. He had been very young and had been in just two years; he had served only a few months of that overseas.

They had several serious discussions about community life during the fall, and each time, Heather was more impressed with his knowledge of the problems confronting a small town which suddenly booms into a city and finds it has growing pains because of its inadequacy to cope with its emergencies.

She had never discussed the house he had spoken of earlier in the summer, because she wished to avoid setting a date for their wedding.

At the office of the Timber Corporation, she occupied a small corner of the main floor until October, when one of the main secretaries, who had formerly worked for Jonathon Nichols, married and left for the East. Her brother immediately gave her the private office and appointed her to the vacancy. Heather liked her new work very much. It gave her additional responsibilities, yet it also gave her more time to take care of them, and she was thrown into administrative work, rather than into the fringe area of routine stenographers' work, which covered typing and statistics and dull office schedules.

Her new boss was the manager whom Marc had employed last year. She found him very serious and businesslike and she liked the atmosphere. He was pleasant but formal with her, and she tried very hard to be efficient.

She was conscious of Seth's disapproval when he asked her, "Does this mean you're going to be a career woman, honey?"

"I'm not making any definite plans, Seth. I'm not even sure that I can be a satisfactory secretary to the manager."

"Isn't that rather taken care of, since you are one of the main stockholders?"

Heather bit her lips. Then she smiled. "Are you implying that I don't really have to be efficient for political reasons?"

"I can imagine that you'd make anyone a very good secretary. Should I feel safer because he's twice your age?" The banter in his voice relieved her, yet she knew that henceforth she would always wonder if Marc had been right in placing her in the position.

She began to learn more about the business than she had ever known before. Queer ports in foreign seas began to have meaning for her as she shifted the pins in the big wall maps when they had messages from their shipments.

South America, the Scandinavian countries, the Balkans, Greece, France, the British Isles, and the Eastern ports of the United States and parts of Mexico became familiar to her on the charts. She attended some of the meetings with foremen from the various plants and learned the terminology of the business world. And by the time Christmas had rolled around, her work had become highly satisfying and challenging to her. She looked forward to it each day as she dressed for the office. She began to wonder if she was treating Seth fairly by delaying their marriage; if it might not drive a wedge between them that could some day irrevocably separate them.

CHAPTER 16

Her brother had begun to date one of the new teachers in November. She was one of the elementary staff, a girl from the South. "A Georgia peach!" Sam had exclaimed upon meeting her when he came home for Thanksgiving. She was a luscious little brunette, small, quite pretty, with a smooth creamy complexion, bright blue eyes and lustrous black hair which she wore rather short in a curly halo about her head. With a delightful accent which pleased the West Coast citizens, she added a great deal to the social life.

"Ah rally do like yo' Miss Shirley," drawled Sam at Christmas. "Ah find her fascinatin' as all get-aout, as do most of the otheh's 'round these pahts. Don' you have some competition, Ma'c?"

His older brother silenced him with a look. But

the twins prattled on unconcernedly. "I think she's the cutest newcomer that ever hit this town," said Janet. "Who'd ever think of her as a teacher? Somehow I always remember Miss Langley when I think of the profession. Straight black hair pulled back so tightly it kept her eyebrows in a perpetual lifted state. A steel-edged voice and gimlet eyes."

"Jane Shirley's eyes are not exactly what you'd expect in a teacher. Did you ever see such lashes? I'm green with envy every time I see her, which is rather often, since she's so popular," said Beverly.

"Gee! It's made no end of an impression on the high school Seniors of the community. I heard that several of them are reconsidering going into teaching. Look at the handsome Physical Ed man at Horace Mann this year. I saw him and Miss Shirley dancing at the Hi-Tide last night. Better look to your laurels, Marc!"

"She's a very nice girl, and not a bit stuffy," he said.

Heather was in her room one evening just before the twins went back to Eugene for the second semester, writing a note at her desk, when Beverly tapped at her door.

"Oh, come on in, Bev," Heather said, laying down her pen.

Her younger sister, dressed in a blue quilted robe, sat down on a corner of the chaise. She was doing her nails, and she spread out the tray of lotions, removers and polish and continued her work.

"Just thought we'd have a little visit, if you're not too busy."

"Glad to lay this aside. I can finish it later," said Heather. "Have to go back to the office this evening, though, to finish a report."

"Aren't you sort of overdoing this office work, Heather? Gee! You've hardly been home during the holidays, and honestly, you've not entered into the spirit at all this year. How does Seth like the idea of your working such long hours?"

"Why, I really don't know, Bev. I've been pretty busy this month getting things ready for inventory. And Marc has had an important board meeting."

"Aren't they all important, to listen to him? Honestly, Heather, you need a shot of some kind. Look at your hair! You need a cut and a permanent. I'm surprised at your not getting fixed up a little more for the New Year's Dance. You didn't even buy a new evening dress this year. You'd not have been caught dead wearing that dress last year!"

Heather laughed lightly. "I'd rather you and

Jan had the new dresses. Really, it's not important."

"I'm not so sure," Beverly tipped her hand up and studied the shade of polish critically.

"Don't beat around the bush! You came in here with a mission. Get along with it, Beverly. I know you twins too well. What's up?"

"I saw Seth and the Georgia peach at lunch to-day."

Heather's heart skipped a beat. "But you went to Dorchester House up at Ocean Lake today, didn't you?"

Beverly nodded. "That's what I'm trying to tell you, honey. Now don't tell me they were on business at Dorchester House."

Heather was silent. Her thoughts were whirling. She had been careless about Seth lately, about keeping their dates and about making plans for having fun. He had asked her to go with him up to the Pagan Hut last Sunday evening, and she had insisted that she'd like to spend the evening with the family, with him included of course. Even then Janet had said, "Don't be silly, Heather. Of course he doesn't want to be entirely surrounded by all of us Nicholses. You're crazy not to go."

Ruefully she admitted that she probably had been a little crazy. "I'd like to get away for a long evening, just you and I, and a good sizzling steak up at the Hut," he had said. She should have realized that it had been a family whirl ever since the twins and Sam had arrived for the holidays. A constant stream of their older friends and some of their newer ones from over in the valley had filled Nichols' Ferry to overflowing.

But Jane Shirley!

Had Seth succumbed to her charms too? What about Marc? And, she thought, wanting to cry suddenly, *What about me?*

A luncheon date at Dorchester House could mean only one thing: that it was a real date, pre-planned. If it had been here in town, they might have happened into the same restaurant at the same time, and sheer coincidence might have thrown them together. But not thirty-five miles up the Coast, on a winter day! She had to concede it had been a beautiful day, though. Bright blue sky, bright blue Pacific. Of course that alone was enough excuse to drive along the edge of the waters and admire them.

"Don't look like that, Heather. It's probably their very first date. You can still do plenty about it."

Heather abruptly moved her hand, and the

diamond in her engagement ring seemed suddenly dimmed. *Maybe I've been a fool to put him off.* Even her mother had said that if she loved Seth, she must not make him wait too long.

She did not answer, and presently she was aware that her sister had left the room so quietly she didn't know how long she'd been gone. She picked up the note she had been writing to a friend in Portland. It was to have been a regret that she and Seth could not come to her wedding on Saturday afternoon. She tore the note in two and reached for the telephone, dialing Seth's home number.

He was not at home, his mother said. Her voice was overly gentle when she asked if there was a message for him. Heather left her name. Putting the receiver back into its cradle, she realized that she didn't have a date with Seth. Not tonight, or any other evening soon.

Then she laughed a little to herself. When had they had need for a date? He usually called late and asked if it would be all right to come out, or if she'd like to go to lunch

Yet why should Seth have asked Jane Shirely to go to lunch with him, unless it was because he wished to be with her? He couldn't help knowing of her brother's interest in Jane, for they had had at least two dates each week on the average the past month. Marc still would not admit that he was serious about Jane, however, and she didn't believe that he had fallen in love with her.

However, she had to remember that her brother was still too concerned with the business to have taken much interest in romance the past few months.

She went down to dinner presently, and tried to act cheerful as though nothing had happened, but she noted that the twins eyed her anxiously several times during the meal. They were off to go dancing at nine, and Heather stayed with her mother in the living room to watch television until ten.

She was anxiously aware that Seth had not called her and she realized that he would probably not call tonight. She sat in front of her dressing table for a long time, trying to remember when there had been even one day that she had not heard from him.

Bleakness descended upon her. An overwhelming feeling that she had lost Seth struck her and when she did go to bed finally, she began to cry. She tried to stop, but sobs began to shake her, and she gave up trying to dry her tears. It had been so long since she had really cried hard about anything, and she knew that she would feel miserable in the morning when she had to go to the office. Finally she got up and went into her bathroom and washed her face and sat by the window. Once she picked up her telephone, then saw that it was one o'clock. With a firm hand she set the receiver down again.

No, Seth would have to make the first approach. He had not seen Beverly and Janet, she supposed, although she had not asked them. Would he tell her that he had lunched with Jane?

The next morning she looked a little pale, but she merely added a little rouge to her make-up and went to work as usual, trying to submerge her depression in the routine of the day. She must get the note written to her friend, either accepting or rejecting the invitation to the wedding. She hadn't even mentioned it to Seth, so she wrote her regrets and sent it out with the mail.

There was no call for her during the day, no little bunch of flowers in the blue vase which Seth usually kept filled for her desk. It was a busy day, and she worked until five-thirty, barely noting that the other employees had left the main office.

Her brother entered her door as she was putting

the cover on her typewriter and said, "Don't you know it's time to go home? You look tired, Sis."

"I've been slaving over a hot desk all day." She managed a smile. "What did you do about your letters? Did you get them off?"

He nodded. "Everything's under control. How about calling Seth? I'll see if I can get Jane, and we can go up to the Pagan Hut tonight for dinner."

The suggestion came as so great a surprise to her that she could think of nothing to say. Then, "Why don't you call Jane first?"

He did so and found her at her small apartment.

"Oh, I see. I know it's late to call you, Jane. If you'll excuse it, please. Yes, yes, I understand. Maybe some other evening soon?"

He replaced the telephone on Heather's desk. "It seems she already had an engagement."

Heather wanted to say, "It was probably with my fiancé," but she refrained. At the moment she put on her coat, her telephone rang, and she dashed back to answer it. Marc had gone on to his car, and she was driving her own, so she sat down, taking a deep breath as she heard Seth's voice.

"Mother said you left a message for me to call," he was saying, measuring his words, it seemed to her. "So many things to see to today that I just now got the chance. Are you busy this evening?"

"No, Seth, I'm not busy. I called last evening to see if you'd like to go to a wedding next Saturday at Portland, but I had to get the answer off, so sent regrets this morning."

"Gee! I'm sorry. We could have gone if you wished."

"I could still call."

"Why don't you do that, if you'd like to go? It's been a long time since we went to Portland together."

They arranged it, and then he said he'd take her out to dinner tonight if she'd like. "Since the Ice Follies are on in Portland, we might stay over Saturday night."

"I think that would be lots of fun," she said. Perhaps there would be time to show him that she cared; perhaps she had not lost him after all.

CHAPTER 17

When they were on their way to Portland to the wedding the following Saturday, Heather reflected that Seth had not mentioned going to lunch with Jane Shirley earlier in the week at Dorchester House. She was trying to think of some way to introduce Jane's name, so that he would be provided with an opportunity.

"Marc and Jane Shirley seem to be quite congenial," she managed finally. "They're going to the Pagan Hut this evening for dinner. I'm glad my brother has finally found someone to interest him. He's worked so hard the past two years."

"All work and no play, you know," said Seth.

"Yes, how true! I've begun to think I should make a New Year's resolution to cut a little off my day's work," she said lightly, "beginning right now!"

"Good for you!" Seth smiled into her eyes. The traffic was particularly heavy at the junction they were approaching, so he kept his eyes on the pavement for several minutes.

"I'm looking forward to seeing the wedding," she said. "Several girls I have known for years will be there."

"It's good to renew acquaintance," he said. "I'm glad we're staying over. The Ice Follies seats I managed to get are quite good. To tell you the truth, I've had them for weeks. Reservations are difficult to get, and when I had the opportunity last month to get them in Portland, I bought them to have just in case."

She was thinking, And what if I'd not agreed to go to the wedding and to stay over? I'd have missed a lovely time with Seth.

He had skipped the opportunity to tell her that he'd lunched with Jane. She could not bring herself to the point of letting him know that the twins had seen them together that day. She resolutely put it from her mind, knowing that if she kept thinking of it, she would let it spoil her whole weekend.

They were so late they drove directly to the church. The wedding was set for four o'clock.

They were ushered into their seats, and found they'd arrived just a few minutes before the tapers were to be lit. The lovely white and pink roses, the tall white tapers and the lovely evergreens made a perfect setting for the pretty bride and the groom, whom Heather had never met.

They went to the house to the reception and, to Heather's delight, she caught the bride's bouquet.

"And with that beautiful diamond on your engagement finger, it won't be very much longer!" cried someone.

She turned to speak to Seth, but he had been talking with the groom, so that she missed the chance to let him know that she might be ready to set their date.

They had dinner at the Chalet before going on to the Ice Follies. She was staying at the Multnomah Hotel, and he at the Heathman, since it was difficult to get reservations. Heather enjoyed the feeling of being in the city again. She had not left Bayport very often during the months since her return there after her Commencement in June, and then usually only for a day's trip into one of the nearby cities.

"Having fun?" Seth asked as she sipped her cocktail before dinner.

"Yes. Are you, Seth?"

"Of course I am, darling. I was just thinking we ought to do this oftener."

She nodded. "One can get in a rut on the Coast. Sometimes we get cabin fever down there and don't even know it."

"This is a fair panacea for it."

He kissed her as he seated her in the car a little later, to drive to the big arena where the Ice Follies were to be presented.

The spectacle was so colorful and thrilling that Heather found herself reliving her first night of the Follies when she was much younger, and had gone with her family. The whole performance had improved immeasurably, delighting the huge audience with each beautiful act.

Many members of the audience were taking moving pictures, capturing for home consumption the beauty of the skaters and the lovely dances which were executed on ice. "The costumes," Heather said, "are simply breath-taking!"

"The very same Follies as are performed at Madison Square Garden in New York," said Seth. "Look at that seventeen-year-old! You'd never guess that she's the youngest in the troupe."

They went to a supper club after the show, and

danced for an hour or so before Seth took her to her hotel. He kissed her in the shadows of the steps, just before they entered the lobby to say goodnight.

"I'm so glad we came," he said.

"I, too, Seth." She pressed his hands briefly. "Breakfast here with me in the morning?"

They arranged to meet at eight-thirty, because they planned on driving up to Timberline Lodge for the day. There would be wonderful skiing, the weatherman had promised.

Weeks later she was glad that she had the memories of the happy weekend to recall: the warmth of the intimate breakfast in the early morning in the dining room before many others had come down to eat; the long, pleasant ride up Mt. Hood to Timberline Lodge with its rustic architecture and the hard-packed snow under the great evergreens.

They wished they'd brought skiing equipment as they watched other people enjoying the trails. Several of Heather's acquaintances were there, and Seth knew two of the men who were ardent skiing enthusiasts.

Heather and Seth had dinner at a nearby inn in the late afternoon, and drove back to Bayport afterward. There was moonlight, and Seth turned the radio on, getting some dance music from the Top O' The Mark in San Francisco. They talked a little about returning to Timberline soon for some skiing, and about driving into Portland to see a new play the following month. Heather felt happy and relaxed as she had not felt for several months.

During the next three weeks they had many pleasant evenings together, and once more Seth's flowers arrived almost daily for the blue vase on her desk; his lunch invitations were frequent, and their companionship was very satisfactory.

Logging camps were operating full time and the weather was in the Nicholses' favor. Long lines of railway flat tops, bearing huge trunks of fir and spruce, rolled into the Nichols yards on schedule; loud splashes from the mill pond accompanied the first step in the processing which kept their giant saws humming.

"Things are really better at the mill, aren't they?" Amy Nichols asked her son one morning.

He sugared his coffee before answering thoughtfully, "Sort of a false sense of security, Mom, I'm afraid. Just before the storm, you know, everything seems calm. No machinery has broken down of late, and that strike was settled amicably, the one I was afraid might extend into our camps. But I keep my fingers crossed." He indicated the gesture.

"Is there anything to cause special anxiety?"

"We lost two of our foremen last week. They went to Pacific, of course. Guess I wouldn't feel so bad if they had left the community, but that they accepted a job with our rivals is hard to take. Has a bad effect on others."

"Offer them more money?"

"Sure," said Marc. "Couple of our old employees with tenure and excellent conditions in their departments. If they'd only come and talked it over with me, I might have managed something to keep them on here."

"Will you be able to replace them?"

Marc nodded. "Just makes us short-handed temporarily, I hope. We're trying to locate someone in Oregon. Of course, we may have a hard time finding anyone close."

In early March the Pacific Timber Corporation opened another plywood mill. And Nichols felt the impact within a week.

"Our men are leaving us like bees swarming after the Queen," said Marc bitterly one evening after office hours.

"I heard it from one of the girls in the main office. Personnel has been making out severance checks most of the day! What does it mean?" Heather covered her typewriter, avoiding the anxious look in her brother's eyes.

"That a lot of our fellows are following those foremen we lost a couple of months ago. I think it's a low, underhanded thing for Pacific to do."

"But it's something the men would naturally have to decide for themselves, Marc. Did you know they were opening up another mill this soon?"

"Of course; it was under construction all winter. We knew we'd have competition in labor, but I didn't realize it would hit us at one of our busiest seasons. We had to close down one department today. Next week we'll probably have to shut down the operations in that whole mill."

"Can't you get other men?"

"Steal them from some other operators?" Marc laughed shortly. "Everything's fair, of course. I'm running a quarter-page ad in the *Oregonian* tomorrow. We should get some results from men who've been laid off, or are too old for better jobs. We can probably get enough to help out until we can do better."

"May I come in?" Paul Nichols stood in the door of Heather's office. "Didn't know you were still here, Heather. I came down the hall to talk to Marc."

"Guess you know what we're talking about, Paul," said Marc. "Have you any more suggestions about the situation?"

"No." Paul sat down in one of the straight chairs reserved for business callers. "As a matter of fact, it hits me pretty hard. I hope you two will understand, but I've been on the verge of asking you to let me go the end of April. I hate even to mention it now, but maybe we can work out something."

Marc said nothing for a full minute; then he lit a cigarette. "I've been expecting you to want to get out all winter, Paul, and I can't blame you. It was good of you to stay on. Are you going over to Pacific, too?"

Paul laughed shortly. "Give me credit for a little loyalty, Cousin Marc. No, on the contrary, I'm going to do just what I want to do for the next six months. I'm sailing for Europe, and am going to spend my time traveling, taking pictures and just having one whale of a time."

"Good for you!" said Marc. "It couldn't happen to a nicer guy, Paul. Looks like we're almost sunk, anyway; maybe if we have to cut operations down, we can at least hold the fort with fewer executives around here."

Heather looked stricken. "What is the cause of all this exodus to Pacific, Paul? Man to man, can you tell us?"

"That's easy. Better working conditions, better money. Hours are a little longer, but the guys get overtime."

Marc strode around the small office. "We've raised our scale until it hurts. You know that, Paul."

His cousin sighed. "No one knows it better. Well, Kids, if you don't mind, I think I'll skip on home for dinner."

"Sure, go ahead. No use to sit around singing the blues here. Won't help any."

After Paul had gone, Heather asked, "Do you think Uncle Jon could give us any advice, Marc?"

Her brother snorted unappreciatively. "Anything from him could not be classified as advice, Heather. You ought to know that! It's still the old squeeze-out. He thinks we should give up. Doesn't Seth ever let you know anything that's going on?"

"We never talk business any more. It spoiled so many evenings together in the beginning. He wouldn't tell me anything that should be kept within their firm!"

"It's no secret that they're paying their men twenty cents an hour more than we do. That adds up to a dollar sixty a day."

"Couldn't you discuss labor problems even with Mr. Barclay? I know he's the Pacific consultant, but nonetheless he's our neighbor and our friend. He might give you some ideas, Marc."

"I'll never ask him for advice, Heather. I'd be a great one to go to him and lay all our cards on the table!"

"But why need it be that way, Marc? Why can't we be friends in business as well as personal friends?"

"Because they struck first, remember!"

"It isn't a question of striking at one another. Other commercial firms have friendly relations with their competitors. I think you're making a mistake, Marc, just ignoring them as you've tried to do," she pleaded.

"Why should I let them have the advantage of knowing our next move? They never inform us!" Marc said bitterly.

CHAPTER 18

Seth ran into Marc at the Kiwanis dinner the following week. He paused in the lobby of the hotel and said, "Nichols, I'm sorry about the mill which had to be closed. Do you have your problem straightened out yet?"

"Not yet." Marc looked as though he had spent some sleepless nights recently. He was not friendly, and Seth sensed that his feelings extended not only to his firm, but to himself personally.

He hesitantly asked, "Is there anything I can do to help?"

"It depends on whose side you're on!" Marc laughed shortly.

"Oh, come now, Nichols. We're civilized people, I hope."

Marc nodded. "I'd thought so, but when we lose

enough of our men to your mills to have to close down one of our main departments, I wonder."

"You know how labor is, Marc. Naturally men go where they can earn higher wages and have better equipment."

"Certainly I understand the cold facts of employment, Barclay. But I've a few cards up my sleeve myself. I'm not taking this sitting down, you know."

"I'm sorry that you're bitter about it, Marc."

"If you were in my shoes, how'd you feel about it?"

"Bitter, too, I guess. But I'd like to give you a hand if I can. I've got a list of men from different sections of the country in our files—they've all been looking for employment. Would you like to go over them, see if you can use any of them?"

"I say, that's darned decent. Yes, I'd like to accept your offer, Barclay."

"Come along with me back to my office, and we'll look over it."

"I have an appointment at two, so if you'd send them over to me, I'd appreciate it."

"Sure thing. I'll bring them myself during the coffee break this afternoon; maybe see my favorite girl."

"Right. Thanks very much for your help." Marc held out his hand and took Seth's, realizing it was the first gesture of real friendship he'd made toward Barclay for many weeks.

The applications were fairly thorough, Marc found when he went over them later. He and the personnel manager went through them together, sifting out the undesirable ones, but getting in touch with many older men with experience in lumber mills. "We often find them more steady and dependable than much younger men," the personnel man said.

Within two weeks the mill had been re-opened, and though their production was far behind schedule and they missed two big shipping dates, Marc was nevertheless grateful to Seth Barclay.

"They are not ruthless and cold, Marc," Heather said a bit triumphantly when she learned about Seth's help.

"You just don't understand big business, Sis."

"Any business is only as cold as its administrators make it seem. The trend today is toward taking a personal interest in public relations; and what could be better relations than our two companies cooperating with each other, helping one another during times of stress, when it's possible?"

"You're an idealist, honey," said Marc. "But you're a pretty good secretary, too."

"When do I get a raise?" she asked playfully.

"*Et tu, Brute?*" He smiled. "Well, it may be sooner now that we're getting back into full production again."

"Do you think we'll catch up with our schedule in time to make a fair showing of profit in the semi-annual report?"

"I do. You know, Heather, you sometimes surprise me. Your knowledge of figures, that is."

"As a college graduate, I can do a little more than add and subtract, Brother. I know that the women of the family are not supposed to worry their little heads about finances, but I've been doing it too long to stop now. Besides, I take pride in knowing something about it."

"Then you'll be pleased to hear that we think we came through our first year after the selling of the other mills with a little profit. We haven't declared dividends yet, but I can assure you that the report will be satisfactory."

"Marc, I think that's wonderful!" Heather walked over to him and, reaching up, kissed him. "I thought when we got so far behind production that we'd take a loss. We missed those two shipments, remember."

"The production manager we hired last year has made a big improvement. I'd not realized how much until we started our reports last week." Her brother took a rapid turn about the office. "Paul was almost worse than nothing in the production department. It was very wise to move him when we did last fall."

She told Seth how pleased she and her brother both were about his helping them. It was one of the few times they had spoken of the mills in the evening.

The next afternoon she was chatting with one of the girls from the main office during their coffee break, when the fire alarm downtown sounded. Immediately afterward they heard the siren from the new mills. For a moment Heather's heart stood still. She thought at first it was from their own. The shrieking signal rose and fell monotonously, proclaiming a big fire.

"Oh, dear! That dreadful sound!" Helen Ashton exclaimed. "I'm always afraid to look out the window." She and Heather raced down the corridor to a large window which faced toward the Pacific Mills, perhaps two miles distant.

The sky above their newest addition was already full of dense smoke, and just as Heather looked out, a burst of flames shot above the roofs.

"There goes an ambulance!" cried Helen. "Someone's been hurt!"

There was the shriek of the ambulance's siren and presently another alarm. Later, two fire trucks from nearby communities went past. The coffee break had ended, but employees kept whispering among themselves. Heather could stand it no longer and went into her brother's office. Marc was gone. And looking about, she discovered that several of the other supervisors had left the plant, too.

Presently she saw a big truck loaded with twenty or thirty Nichols men, speeding down their wide drive toward the gates. Upon seeing them, she went to the parking lot and took her car and drove quickly toward the Pacific Mills.

A traffic policeman stopped her two blocks from the burning building. "Can't go any farther, Miss Nichols. Better go back and park over by the Dutch Treat."

"Okay. Thanks, Officer Dooley." She started to turn, then drove up beside him and asked, "How bad is it?"

"Pretty bad, I'm afraid. Two men seriously injured, three killed. It was an explosion, and one of those new scientists from the East was hurt pretty bad. Not much chance for him, I guess."

"How terrible!"

"Nichols men are helping move out some of the smaller, valuable equipment. A lot of the Pacific men were off today, because the plant was installing some new equipment. Left 'em shorthanded to fight the fire. It's spread to four of the smaller buildings and to the largest in that new unit."

Heather shook her head. She drove on slowly to avoid other cars, and wished that she'd left her car blocks away, for she couldn't get out of a lane.

It was after dark before the fire was completely under control, and she felt sick when she heard that one of the injured men had died. She tried to call Seth, but was unable to reach him. She was very anxious. Had Seth been in the office? She felt she had to see him, touch him, find out that he was all right.

She called his home; his mother had talked with her husband only ten minutes before.

"They're both all right, Heather, my dear. It's been ghastly, but we can be thankful that the whole crew was not in that building when the explosion occurred. The flash fire which resulted might have killed many of them."

"Is there any thing I can do to help?"

"You know, I can't drive, and I have gallons of coffee and lots of sandwiches made up. Do you think—?"

"I'll be right over to help you. We can take them as far as the entrance, I think. The patrol wasn't letting anyone through the lines, but it's better now, I believe."

"So good of you," Mrs. Barclay said.

Knowing her own mother would be anxious to hear, Heather called and reassured her. Amy had heard from Marc and was feeling very sad about the trouble at the Pacific plant. "Those poor fellows! You know the man who died was one of Seth's schoolmates. He just arrived last week."

"How awful!" Heather kept thinking of it while she drove to the Barclay's to get Seth's mother. She found that Mrs. Barclay had been crying.

"That poor young man! I know how horrible Seth will feel, for he got him to come out here to do some work for them developing a new gluing process for the new plywood they're getting ready to manufacture. He and Seth both majored in Wood Technology," Mrs. Barclay said.

Heather put her arm about her. "You mustn't worry, though it's terribly tragic."

"I know my husband observes all safety practices, and the equipment is very fine; he's very conscious of working conditions, you know."

When they arrived with the coffee and sandwiches, they found that some of the Nichols men were still helping move the machinery which had been saved into storage spaces in other buildings.

It was nine o'clock before she saw Seth. He was rumpled and haggard. He was almost distracted with anxiety when he saw her, and though she tried to comfort him, he said bitterly, "I'm responsible for his death! How can I ever face his wife?"

She was arriving by plane tomorrow morning, and he was going to meet her. Heather knew what a task that would be. "Alan was such a fine person. He has a lovely wife, and they're expecting a baby, their first. Isn't it awful, Heather?"

"Would you like me to go with you to meet her?"

"Would you, Heather? Would you, dear?"

"I most certainly will, Seth." She put her arm about his waist.

Gratefully, he stooped and kissed her, and she

could suddenly smell the odor of smoke and
scorched wood and see that his hair had been
singed a little.

"You worked in that burning building, didn't
you?" she asked.

"Well, certainly. I wouldn't stand outside and
let Nichols men go in to work alone, would I?
They probably saved the building next to it, for
they worked like beavers. You should have seen
them! A lot of fire fighters—service men, you
know. They know their business. No, I'd say if it
wasn't for our good friends from the Nichols
mills, we'd probably be completely out of business!"

She brushed off his forehead with her white
linen handkerchief and brushed back his dry hair.

He tucked her hand in his arm and propelled
her to the car. "We at Pacific are greatly indebted
to Nichols. I doubt if we can ever repay you,
Heather."

"Oh, well, maybe it's another step in better relations; remember, you helped us out of a bad
situation last month!"

CHAPTER 19

Oregon in April was something to behold, people kept telling each other, especially those who lived along the Coast. Alders, willows, the elderberry clumps along the highways and by-ways were growing inches each day; the brilliant yellow blooms of skunk cabbage thrust their lily-like spikes into hundreds of meadows; and low creek and river bottom lands and the brilliant rose of wild currants combined to enrich the kaleidoscopic colors. Blue skies above and the blue waters of the Pacific added their technicolor intensity.

Each day she viewed this unbelievable beauty, Heather told herself that the troubles at their plants were balanced by the restful landscape, that a man could stand the burdens of worry, if from time to time he could just get away from the offices and look at the countryside. Away from the town, one could forget the din of traffic and mill whistles, the crowded condition of the narrow streets where one could no longer secure a parking place.

Heather and Amy attended one of the early April Citizens' Committee Meetings. Several projects were discussed, among them the need for more school buildings to supplement those built last year.

"Along with our increased payroll at the mills, naturally come shopkeepers of all kinds, so that Bayport has increased its population by leaps and bounds the past ten months," said the chairman. "By actual statistics, we have more than quadrupled our school population. Large families seem to be the order of the day once more."

Amy whispered, "How true! That new family moving in yesterday down the road has five children, and all of them are of school age."

Heather smiled, remembering the number in her own family. It did seem true that many of the girls with whom she had gone to High School had more than one or two children. "Suah does increase the average daily attendance," said Jane Shirley one evening. "Why, ouh fi'st graders are now occupying six rooms instead of three!" The average daily attendance wasn't the only thing to reckon with. The unit system had to maintain a transportation system, and school buses could not be bought for peanuts.

"Some of our buses, in fact more than half of them, are fifteen and sixteen years old!" said the director, in a talk before the P.T.A. "We couldn't possibly keep our attendance up if we hadn't good mechanics who are trained to take care of the school buses, which I wish to assure you are entirely different from family cars!" Heather knew that the men sometimes had to work all night to put in a new engine, or to make extensive repairs to keep the buses rolling the next day, for there were none in reserve to replace them.

"The old worn out buses, the murderous county roads, some of them not much better than old logging roads, make transporting children costly."

The annual budget election was to be held the following week, and to get the lethargic people to the polls, it was decided to help the P.T.A. transport voters who had no means of getting there.

"It is especially necessary to get the budget adopted. Every time we hold an election, it costs the people tax money. We have trimmed the budget to the bone, and we cannot attack the bones themselves lest the structure fall."

Heather listened attentively to the rest of the discussion. There were many things brought up. Someone suggested they try to get the Council to pass a smoke ordinance against the mills. The suggestion was put into the form of a motion, seconded and passed.

"Just because we're having fine weather right now, and the heat hasn't started up in the valley yet to send the fog rising here, we must not forget our troubles of the past."

"I'll say not!" cried one housewife, springing to her feet. "I live out near that new mill which opened up last month. I can't dry my clothes outdoors any more, and we have to buy an expensive dryer—just so the Pacific Mills can blow their old smoke all over creation!" She glared at the others. "If you men think housekeeping in Bayport is easy these days, you ought to try keeping windows and curtains clean, not to say anything about the white stone of that new church!"

"Hear! Hear!" said the Mayor affably. "Steps are being taken to try to do something about the smoke."

"Yeah! That's what you said last year! Along

about November, I remember."

"That's right!" chimed in one or two women.

"Well, Ladies, we're going to do something positive right away. You can count on it."

"Must be running for reelection," someone behind her said in a stage whisper, and several people laughed heartily.

"Promises!" hissed the first speaker as she sat down.

The Mayor mopped his brow.

"It must be tough to try to keep everyone happy," said the chairman. "After all, we wanted the big payrolls here in the community. Naturally new industry brings many problems along with it."

"It sure does!" exclaimed one of the businessmen from the waterfront. "Excuse me, Ladies! When do we get that pipeline ditch finished that's been gumming up the works for us? That street was torn up last year on account of the new sewer, and this year I guess we'll be holding the sack again! Well I lost thousands last year, but I'm going to ride the horse differently this time."

"Let's get on the ball and get something done in this community," said one of the younger fathers. "It's sickening to hear talk, talk, talk, and no action.

I'll work on a committee, Mr. Mayor; in fact I'll head one for any of the major projects you've mentioned here tonight. We younger people have to get out and get a hump on. It's our families who are cluttering up the schools anyway. I'll have four children in grade school next year. They've got as good a right to an education as the next kid, say in Portland or Eugene, where they pay the teachers excellent salaries and the buildings are built when they're needed!" He turned around and faced the audience. "Don't you ever get sick of listening to some old-timer or a thwarted politician talking about the good old days?" He thrust out his jaw, shook his finger and shouted:

"I went to school right over there, in the old Mill Bottom schoolhouse. We had a pot-bellied stove in every room and a dangling bulb for light. And though we had some teachers who were good in the old days before World War II, we in this unit often had to take the dregs because teachers who didn't actually live here wouldn't teach under such conditions unless they couldn't find jobs elsewhere."

He suddenly strode from his seat and went to the front of the room. "I've been wanting to get some things off my chest for a long time, and this seems to be as good a time as any. If any of you want your children to go back to those old days, you might as well leave right now, for you're not going to like what I say. If any of you're willing to trade in your family car right now for an old horse and buggy, say so. Otherwise, you've no right to subject our kids to that kind of treatment. You with your beer taverns on every corner, your fat checks from the mills, and time and a half for overtime. Who ever paid a teacher for grading hundreds of papers in the evening when you're down at a bar or hunched over your television sets? Who among us would try to take on as many as forty-nine or fifty different children a year, to guide and teach and work with them? Why, we can't handle four or five or even two or one of our own sometimes. You bellyache when the schools close a day for 'Institute' or 'In-Service Training,' 'cause your own kids get on your nerves!"

There was no sound as he paused.

"I know, because I've heard you. I know because I've done it myself. Now, I say, it's time to shut up and go to work! How many of you're going to that meeting next week and take two or three friends that you KNOW will vote for the budget?"

There was a wild roar of applause.

"Who *is* he, Mother?" whispered Heather.

"A new young William Jennings Bryan, if you ask me!" smiled Amy happily. "A reformer. It had to happen, or this whole area would have been wretchedly sunk!"

After the shouting died down, Heather rose to her feet. "I work every day, but I'm anxious to give some of my time to help out in any way that I can. I volunteer my services right now to supply stenographic help of any kind needed."

As she sat down, she heard a deep masculine voice from the back of the room. It was Seth! She turned, and saw his tall, straight figure, observed his smile as he said, "I think that's most commendable of Miss Nichols. I, too, will be happy to devote some of my leisure time, as our friend just said, to 'get on the ball' and help out. We can either make or break our community life. A city is just what the citizens make of it. I'll help, if I may, or at least try to help."

Later, as the meeting broke up, Heather and Amy went toward the little crowd who were surrounding the young father who had been so outspoken. Heather heard Seth's words as he shook hands with him. "You did a great job, Mike. It takes your kind to get things started."

Mike was wiping his face. "I'd never have had the guts if it hadn't been for you, Barclay. You put the words in my mouth this afternoon when we had our coffee break down at the mill."

Seth? Heather was staring at him, wide-eyed. How could he have been so influential? A great warmth overcame her, and when she could, she managed to slip up to him and whispered, "You're simply wonderful, Seth! I heard what Mike said about your egging him on!"

Seth held her hand for a moment. "We've got a lot to do, and I'm glad that you're going to help us!" He looked for Amy, who had begun to speak to a bystander. "How about letting your mother go home in your car, and joining me after this is over? We've got a big full moon tonight. Wouldn't you like to help me go bay at it?"

She smiled and nodded.

CHAPTER 20

The younger parents organized a house to house canvas to create interest in community problems, and specifically to get the people out to vote. Community service clubs, the Lions, Kiwanis, Rotary, Toastmasters, women's clubs, church organizations, the Business and Professional Women's Club, the P.E.O., and A.A.U.W. and one or two study groups all got busy. As a consequence more voters than had ever turned out for a school budget election proudly adopted the budget by a landslide.

"And if we can do it for our schools, we can do it for our road and housing problems and the other problems which confront us," said Mike Taylor, who had done so much to get the activities started.

The Pacific Mills had rebuilt their plywood building and the other three small buildings within three months, so that they were operating at full production again.

The Nichols Timber Corporation was solidly on its feet by August, and Marc and Sam sometimes talked about the possibilities of expansion in the future.

Heather, listening to them discuss this, felt it sounded much like history repeating itself, as she recalled listening to her father and grandfather talk by the hour when she was small. Occasionally she took out a huge scrap book she had once made for her father one winter, with clippings, and old photographs of the early railway which terminated at Yaquina and the Lollypop, the little pleasure boat which plied back and forth between Yaquina City and Bayport.

"I well remember the day the Governor and his guests came from the Capitol to dedicate the cornerstone of the first school building here on the Coast," her grandfather had said. "When they raze that old building over in the pasture some day, they'll find some interesting things in the cornerstone. We scratched our names or initials in the coins we put into it, and the Corvallis *Gazette* of that week published a story about the dedication. It's there, too."

At a meeting of the Historical Society, she told those attending that the old bell, the contents from the cornerstone and some old papers were available for their archives, or for the museum they hoped to build sometime.

"Why build a museum when the old lighthouse would be perfect for it?" said Seth. "In the East they restore such valuable landmarks as the old lighthouse. Out here in the Northwest, we burn them! What Philadelphia or New York would give for such an inspiring structure! Your tourists would flock in and pay a small fee to go through it."

Everyone knew the lighthouse to which he referred. Built in 1872, it had been used only a year or two because its beams did not reach far enough out to sea. A higher promontory was chosen and a new one built farther up the Coast at Cape Foulweather, named for its gusty winds and bleak position.

"You know, Seth," Heather remarked later after the meeting, "you're apt to be the most popular man in the community with the exception of Mike Taylor, if you keep this up."

"Or the most unpopular one!" he amended. "I can hear the Taxpayers' Association tearing me and my suggestions apart. Actually, to sustain the lighthouse would cost only the price of one or two beers a year per taxpayer."

"There are many who'd rather have the beer," he pointed out. "We tried to raise money for a museum twice before, but got no results from the voters."

"If we try it again in a couple of years, after some of these other community problems are worked out, maybe it can be put across. Actually, I've heard from the county engineer that the old lighthouse, built of redwood, will stand, with a few minor repairs, for another hundred years. It would be a crying shame to raze it."

They were driving along the Bay in the late afternoon of a beautiful September Sunday. Heather, sitting close to Seth, thought there was no more beautiful time than September on the Oregon Coast. The mist was beginning to rise in the distance, above the firs outlining the far shore, and the sun was casting its final beams in the western sky.

Seth took one of her hands and, turning his head, looked deep into her soft blue eyes. "Do you

ever think of us, Heather? You seem to be eternally
absorbed in office routine, or in the community
problems which submerge almost everyone these
days. What about us?" His eyes were on the road
again.

Her heart began to pound. It had been weeks
since he'd even suggested that they look for a
house, weeks since he'd said anything about marriage. And it's been my own fault, too, she had
told herself of late.

Now, moving closer to him in the car, she put
her fingers up over his long tanned ones. "Yes,
Seth, I do think of us. I realize that I've let many
things come between us—little things which I
thought were important. And yet, to my chagrin,
I've known for a long time that we were really in
accord on most things." It would be difficult to
admit that her brother's feeling of rivalry had
almost destroyed hers and Seth's chances for a
happy marriage.

"I think you proved long ago that we could
be on friendly terms—your company and ours—
without injuring each other, and I believe your
helping us out of our unemployment predicament
was the turning point in our business relations."

Seth said seriously, "But why wouldn't we try

to help? It was our firm which was responsible for the situation. We can both enjoy success in this great country; in fact, there's plenty of room for other concerns to build here."

"I know. Just because we—our grandfather, that is—got here first is no sign there's no room for anyone else." Heather and her brother had discussed all of this not more than a week ago. "Actually, we hear that a new plywood and pulp mill is to be built over in the Siletz area next summer."

Seth nodded. "Rumors get around fast, don't they! It's a Seattle firm, I understand. Guess both Nichols and Pacific will need to look to their laurels!"

Heather's thoughts were not solely on the mills, though, but on how much she loved Seth and how nearly she had lost him. "My brother and Jane Shirley are waiting at the house to take us out to dinner," she said.

"In that case, what do you say we turn off here and go the long way home?" Seth pulled the car toward the left to make a turn. "I want to show you something and get your opinion."

"Fine. Just so we're not too late. I forgot to tell you that they've asked us to go out with them to the Hi-Tide."

"Seven-thirty be all right?" he asked, glancing at his watch. He began to slow down about two miles from the junction, and turned up another road, newly paved. They passed two houses, spaced a quarter of a mile or so apart.

She noticed a new house upon the little hill to the right. "Seth, isn't that a darling house? I look at it every time I pass here. See those lovely wide windows overlooking the Bay, and the curving drive and those beautiful trees!"

"Shall we turn in and look at it?"

"Just for a few minutes. I guess there's time."

The paving had just been finished, she knew; she recalled seeing the mixers and graders there last week. A car was in the garage, she noted. "Oh, I didn't know anyone had moved in," she said.

"I don't think anyone has. Must be a real estate salesman. In fact, Heather, he agreed to meet me here, so I could show you through."

"Oh, Seth!" Her blue eyes were shining. "You had it planned."

"It's yours, darling, if you like it. There can be some changes in decoration or anything but major structure. It's a beauty, and has more space than you can realize from the road."

Built of redwood and brick, with large thermopaned windows, a patio and landscaped grounds, the house was beautiful. Heather fell in love with it. There were three spacious bedrooms and a small guest room or den, a long beam-ceilinged living room with a dining ell; and the kitchen was a modern miracle of steel cabinets, built-in range and refrigerator, formica, brass and colorful tile.

The salesman followed them from room to room, pointing out the assets of central heating, insulation, termite shields, triple plumbing and utility space.

"It's just perfect," Heather whispered to Seth as they tried to lose the salesman. They had paused in the entrance hall to try out the chimes.

"And you'd settle for this to start our married life? We can build another one later, if you want a larger, handsomer one."

Heather's silvery laugh rang out. "Or build onto it, as we did at Nichols' Landing year after year." She could see an imaginary small boy peeping around the corner of the fireplace and two little girls in white ruffled pinafores sitting on the hall steps. "Strangely," she said aloud, "they look like you, Seth."

As though he knew exactly what she meant, he added, "But the girls have your beautiful blue eyes, darling, and the boys' knees are skinned just as mine always were."

They kissed in the dim light of the hall, and Heather clasped her arms about his neck. "I love you so much, Seth. You didn't have to bribe me with the house, you know."